Other 1632 Universe Publications

1632 by Eric Flint created this universe. Free download available at Baen .com/1632.html. Available at Baen.com.

Short-List of Titles to Jump into the Series:

Ring of Fire anthology edited by Eric Flint

1633 by Eric Flint and David Weber

1634: The Baltic War by Eric Flint and David Weber

All books available through Baen.com, booksellers, and used bookstores.

Also Available:

Grantville Gazette Volumes 1 – 102, magazine edited by Eric Flint, Paula Goodlett, Walt Boyes, Bjorn Hasseler. Available on 1632Magazine.com.

1632 Universe novels and "Eric Flint, Ring of Fire Series" on Baen.com

Recently Released and Forthcoming:

1637: The French Correction by Eric Flint and Walter Hunt

1637: The Pacific Initiative by Iver P. CooperOngoing: Baen is re-releasing select 1632 books originally released by Eric Flint's Ring of Fire Press, starting with Bjorn Hasseler's NESS books. Please check the Baen.com e-arc bundles and new releases regularly!

Odd numbered months: New issues of Eric Flint's 1632 & Beyond

Reading Order:

There are three different reading orders available. The first is chronological. The second is by storyline. The third is by publication date.

https://author.1632magazine.com/canon-continuity/reading-order-small-bites/

Issue #14 November 2025

Eric Flint's

1632
& Beyond

David Hankins

Virginia DeMarce

Terry Howard

John Deakins

Natalie Silk

Bjorn Hasseler

Tracy S. Morris

ERIC FLINT'S 1632 & BEYOND #14

This is a work of fiction. Names, characters places, and events portrayed in this book are fictional or used fictitiously. Any resemblance to real people (living or dead), events, or places is coincidental.

Editor-in-Chief Bjorn Hasseler
Production and Design Bethanne Kim
Editor Chuck Thompson
Cover Artwork by Cortney Skinner
Interior Art Garrett W. Vance

1. Science Fiction-Alternate History
2. Science Fiction-Time Travel

eBook ISBN: 978-1-962398-31-2
Paperback ISBN: 978-1-962398-32-9

Distributed by Flint's Shards Inc.
339 Heyward Street, #200
Columbia, SC 29201

Contents

Eric Flint's 1632 & Beyond

Issue 14

This issue was not planned with a theme. Nor did I pick stories because they matched. In fact, I didn't even notice until the stories were back from the proofreaders. Every single one answers the question, "Whatever happened to _____?"

Magdeburg Messenger
(Fiction)

Twenty-five years ago, in Chapter 4 of *1632*, Balthazar and Rebecca Abrabanel's carriage driver fled. David Hankins tells the driver's story in "The Abrabanel Rescue." This is David's first 1632 story.

"The Arabian Queen" by Virginia DeMarce follows characters who've had a much shorter wait, picking up right after "The Play's The Thing" from Issue 11.

Terry Howard's "More McDonalds" also follows a story from Issue 11, "Clan McDonald." This concludes that arc, although not the story of the McDonald clan.

"Artists From Afar" by John Deakins is the sequel to "Chiaroscuro" from *Grantville Gazette* 89.

Anya's story continues in "Green, Blue, and Bruises." Natalie Silk first introduced Anya in *Grantville Gazette* 87, and some members of her family appeared as recently as Issue 12.

Redbird Reader
(Fiction)

"Guardians of Germany" by Bjorn Hasseler takes place largely at Redbird Institute. It draws together Wilhelm Reuber (*Grantville Gazette* 61), the missing fourth von Hesler brother (*Grantville Gazette* 56), and Sunshine Moritz (*Security Solutions*).

The State Library Papers
(1632 Non-Fiction)

Twenty-five years isn't just a long time for characters. It's a long time for authors, too. When the Ring of Fire happened on Sunday, April 2, 2000, the world was a very different place than it is today. Tracy Morris provides us with reminders of what electronic entertainment was like, in "Movies and Television The Year Before The Ring of Fire."

Before we get to the stories, we have a brief survey to see what you would like. Please follow your choice of link or QR code to let us know what you want.

Baen Press Release

Baen.com/pr-eric-flint-1632

For Immediate Release
Baen Books Continues Publishing Eric Flint's "1632" Novels

RIVERDALE, NEW YORK, OCTOBER 17, 2025 – Toni Weisskopf has announced the Baen Books will be publishing more books in Eric Flint's 1632 series.

In accordance with Eric's wishes, Chuck Gannon has been named the series' "showrunner." That role includes oversight and development of all physically published content, managing the series' thematic directions, and close consulting on cross-platform opportunities and marketing.

Gannon brings broad experience and achievements to his role, both as an editor and a best-selling author. A four-time Nebula finalist (novel), he is also the recipient of the American Library Association Choice Award for Outstanding book, the Dragon Award, and the Compton Crook Award.

His work with other writers has been diverse, including: script/story doctor for feature films; developmental editor for the Ring of Fire and other fiction/RPG properties; senior editor for journals in his roles as a Fulbright Fellow; and Program Director of a Minor in Creative Writing focused on fiction for main-stream markets. As a Featured Speaker, he annually brings these varied skills to the Superstars Writing Seminar, in addition to workshops in world building, collaborative authorship, and cross platform IP development.

The next two releases in the 1632 series are the last that Eric proposed, shaped, and contracted with Baen. The first is *1637: The Pilgrim's Passage* by Eric Flint & Griffin Barber, the third in the Mughal India thread. After that comes *1637: Their Finest Hour*, a mainline novel by Chuck Gannon which draws in major characters and elements from the Caribbean thread.

Further development of these and other arcs is underway, but Baen is not yet accepting unsolicited submissions for the Ring of Fire. In the meantime, new, prospective writers should familiarize themselves with the series' novels, as well as the magazine *1632 & Beyond*. All are available as ebooks at Baen.com.

Speaking about this impending re-expansion of the series, Gannon remarked, "Eric's passing was a deeply personal blow to all of us. But his generous spirt and unique vision continues to guide our journey—as well as that of the uptimers and downtimers whose lives were forever transformed by his Ring of Fire.

"Lastly, it's impossible to overstate the importance of his readers' loyalty and enthusiasm since losing him. Their patience was crucial as we worked toward the moment when Baen could make today's announcement: that Eric Flint's *1632* is moving forward at the charge!"

For more information, visit **Baen.com**, email **info@Baen.com**, or call **1-800-ITS-BAEN**.

******

www.Baen.com

1632 Interest Survey
Conventions & Beyond

Science fiction & fantasy has conventions where fans gather to meet their favorite authors. 1632 minicons began with Eric Flint guiding other writers around Mannington, West Virginia, the model for Grantville. After a few years, the 1632 minicon became a track within another convention, moving from convention to convention to provide opportunities to fans in different geographic areas.

Please follow either this link or the QR code and answer these questions to help us plan. We want to bring 1632 to you. You can also find a link to the survey on our blog at https://blog.1632magazine.com/interestsurvey/

Example Questions:

Would you attend a science fiction/fantasy convention with a 1632 track ("minicon")?

How far are you willing to travel for this?

How important is easy site access via plane, train, or bus?

May we have your ZIP code for convention planning purposes?

Which 1632 Baen plotlines or threads would you like to see more of?

From which 1632 Baen authors would you like to read more books?

Which 1632 & Beyond plotlines or threads would you like to see more of?

From which 1632 & Beyond authors would you like to read more books?

Patreon Supporters

1632 & Beyond thanks the following Patreon members who have generously agreed to help underwrite the magazine's operations.

Thank you so much for supporting us.

Gary
Pascal Durand
Marc Foppen
Sally Hardwick
Karjala Koponen
Jerry Johnson
Marc Tyrrell
David Smith
Edh Stanley
Campbell Menzies
Thomas Williams
Virginia DeMarce
Jay Robison
Chuck Thompson

The Magdeburg Messenger

(fiction)

Flint's Shards, Inc.

The Abrabanel Rescue
By David Hankins

The Abrabanel Rescue
David Hankins

This story begins alongside Chapter 4 of 1632.

Dominik Wagner was not a brave man on his best days, and today was definitely not his best day. Yet still he followed the tracks of his stolen coach through the budding Thuringian forest, escaping the carnage behind him while chasing a danger he did not understand. Herr Abrabanel and his daughter needed him. He wouldn't abandon them again.

His footsteps were nearly silent on the forest's soft loam. Birds sang overhead and squirrels chattered, unaware and uncaring of the war that had ravaged their landscape for over a decade now. The wind sighed through the trees. It promised peace while chasing Dominik with the coppery stench of blood. He shuddered. *So much blood.*

Despite driving Balthazar and Rebecca Abrabanel halfway across war-ravaged Germany, the bodies at the massacre he'd just fled were the first he'd seen up close. The Landsknecht guards Herr Abrabanel had hired as escorts had done well up to today, before a band of Tilly's mercenaries saw the carriage and gave chase. Still, they might have escaped if the mounted guards hadn't turned them onto the track to that fateful farmyard. The soldiers had reined in sharply when they saw the massacre: more of Tilly's men—all dead—and judging from the motionless bodies, the farmer and his wife. Only the killers remained standing, well-armed noblemen with their weapons aimed at the coach. The Landsknecht guards had taken one look at the scene and run, taking Dominik's courage with them.

To his shame, he'd abandoned his six-horse coach, sure that the Abrabanels were right behind him. Who would stay to face men who killed while wearing fancy black and white silks? Especially when more of Tilly's mercenaries were so close behind. Yet the doctor and his daughter hadn't followed. They never left the coach. In his fear, Dominik had abandoned them to the murderous noblemen's dubious mercies.

At least, he thought they were noblemen. Their clothes were odd but high quality, and their guns were unlike anything he'd ever encountered. Small, sleek, and deadly. Within minutes of Dominik abandoning his coach, the chasing mercenaries had thundered up to the farmyard. The nobles killed them to a man. The sound of those impossible rapid-shooting guns still rang in Dominik's ears. Once the fight was over, they'd stolen Dominik's coach and kidnapped his passengers.

Dominik pushed the memories down, nearly tripping over a rabbit hole in his distraction. *Focus on the trail*. What did these nobles want with the Abrabanels?

"Ransom," he answered quietly to himself. That was the only logical explanation. Balthazar was a doctor from the wealthy Abrabanel family. He would fetch a high ransom. But negotiations across the continent would take months. Months of captivity for the gentle old man and his beautiful daughter. Dominik had no children; his wife died in childbirth eighteen years ago, and he'd never remarried. But if he'd had a daughter, he'd have wanted one like Rebecca, smart and self-possessed. He'd thoroughly enjoyed debating philosophy and religion with her and her father in the evenings during their journey from Amsterdam.

And that was what drove him onward. Most passengers were nothing but a fare. But the Abrabanels had been different. Though much better educated, they had treated him as an equal. Unlike the minor nobility and rich merchants he normally drove around, they had been kind. Rebecca, in particular, had been charm itself.

Dominik shuddered. What would happen to her in captivity? True, nobles wouldn't be as brutal as Tilly's mercenaries would have been. At least, he didn't think so. They'd even left men behind to bury the dead, which indicated a modicum of honor. But still, a young woman in captivity...

This was his fault. He never should have stopped the coach, despite the guards reining in sharply in front of his team. He should have driven on.

* * *

An hour later, Dominik was no longer confident that the Abrabanels' captors were nobility. At least, not all of them. He didn't know what they were, but his Protestant soul was leaning toward "spawn of the Devil." He didn't think he'd stumbled into hell; this didn't look like one of hell's nine circles from Dante's *Inferno*, but witchcraft was clearly at work.

He lay among low bushes on the climbing edge of a steep gully that half-surrounded an empty parade field. Beyond the field, squatting on a small rise among gentle hills, was the most peculiar facility he'd ever seen. It was white and beige and large enough to be an Amsterdam merchant's warehouse, though more sprawling. A small crowd milled outside an entrance on the right side of the long building, but his focus was transfixed by the smooth black courtyard that filled the space between the parade field and the facility. Its surface was composed of pebbles and tar, of all things, and crisscrossed by yellow lines. He'd walked for a mile or so down a similarly paved road to get here. What captured his attention, though—and convinced him that he was witnessing witchcraft—were the strange coaches squatting in the courtyard. They were metal and shiny, in garish colors, set with impossibly perfect glass windows—and moved without horses. Several had departed, and one had returned, driven by the locals. When they passed his hiding place near the edge of the road, he heard them growl like hungry beasts.

It was magic, which any good Christian knew was evil. He'd been almost painfully pious in the decades since his mother had decided that private sermons from a priest were the best way to reform her wayward child. From everything he'd been taught, this was a place abandoned by God.

The only familiar sight amidst the bizarre tableau was his coach and team parked near the entrance of the building. His horses, at least, seemed unconcerned by their surroundings. They were a good team.

A large sign at the entrance to the facility was indecipherable but for one word. This was a school. He shook his head. It didn't look anything like the recently established Athenaeum Illustre in Amsterdam. Much too big.

Regardless, the Abrabanels must be inside. Captives. Worry for them made Dominik feel sick. Now he would have to rescue them from the spawn of the Devil.

God help him.

It had been years—decades really—since he'd practiced the art of infiltration, and then his only opponent had been the surly baker next door. The man was a genius with pretzels, but he'd had a mean streak when it came to children. He'd start bellowing anytime the much younger Dominik had stepped into his bakery.

One summer long before this wretched war, Dominik had decided to steal a pretzel a day from the old troll to share with his friends. It had been glorious! The baker almost caught him a dozen times, but Dominik developed a knack for remaining just out of sight. His friends had called him *der Brezelgeist*—the pretzel ghost.

It was his mother who finally caught him enjoying his ill-gotten prize with two friends. That was the end of *der Brezelgeist*. She'd made him work for that miserable baker for a month to pay back what he'd stolen—and she made him confess to the priest. He'd never forget those lectures. The Protestant priest had been terrifyingly explicit about the fate awaiting thieves and sinners. He'd never stolen again.

Now those self-taught lessons in infiltration surfaced as Dominik surveyed the school. Or, more precisely, as he surveyed the people milling about outside the school. It appeared to be a post-wedding celebration, judging from their fancy attire. The men and boys wore similar outfits on a theme, mostly black and white, but the women! Only a handful wore respectable dresses. The rest showed more skin than an Amsterdam prostitute or even—most scandalous—wore skin-tight garments. They may as well have been naked.

"Who cares how they're dressed, Dominik," he muttered. "How do you get past them?"

Several of the young women were gathered around the coach, fawning over Dominik's horses. Their delighted voices carried across the courtyard and parade field in accented English. The men at the farmhouse had spoken the same, a language of which Dominik only understood basic phrases. He'd never heard of an English enclave in Germany. He shook his head. It was all too much!

Focus, Dominik. Find a way inside.

He drew a deep breath. He couldn't go through the front door. Some of the milling men had those infernal rapid-fire guns. He had no weapons beyond a general-purpose knife no longer than his palm. Stealth would be his weapon. He scanned the building.

There! The facility was mostly surrounded by the black-paved courtyard and close-shorn grass, though Dominik didn't see any sheep. However, the rear of the building seemed to back up to the dense forest and a steep hillside. He'd have to circle around to reach it without being seen, but losing time was worth avoiding the risk of capture. He'd sneak in, find the cell where the Abrabanels were held, and sneak out. His coach out front would be their escape. With surprise, he could break from the crowd and be down the marvelously smooth road before anyone could mount a pursuit. It wasn't much of a plan, but nothing better came to mind.

Not feeling confident at all, Dominik scrambled back down the gully. Once the scratchy underbrush hid him from view, he ran half-crouched along the gully's base.

He emerged from the woods behind the school. *Nobody around.* The woods didn't quite reach the back of the building, but there was a door propped open next to large metal bins that smelled of midden. With an anxious sprint, Dominik charged across the small expanse of black and then flattened himself against the brick wall beside the door. It was cool and oddly light-colored, not red. He paused, breath loud in his ears, heart pounding in his chest. He listened.

No cry of alarm.

He poked his head inside and saw only a dark hall lined with doors. He slipped inside. The first doors he passed were open and led to a dark kitchen. Beyond that, the doors were inset with glass windows and closed. He peeked through one of the windows. Why was nothing lit? There were no lanterns, candles, or even torches that he could see. The building was obviously occupied, based on the crowd out front, but the interior felt abandoned.

So, where do you keep prisoners in a semi-abandoned building?

Footsteps echoed from an intersecting hallway. Dominik froze. His heartbeat felt like war drums summoning the enemy. He pushed the door lever and slipped silently inside. Well, almost silently. His boots insisted on squeaking softly on the smooth floor. He dropped below the window, breath held.

His knee bumped a small, round, metal bin. It wobbled with a low *wop-wop* sound. Dominik scrambled to catch it, swallowing a curse. He caught it with two fingers, but then he overbalanced and fell onto his side with a grunt. He lay in the darkness, not daring to move, barely daring to breathe.

The footsteps neared and then passed without pausing, male voices engaged in tense conversation. He didn't catch much of their English but understood two words. "Balthazar" and "attack."

That didn't sound good. Had Herr Abrabanel fought back? The old man wouldn't have stood a chance against his captors, especially not against the broad-shouldered nobleman who seemed to be their leader.

The footsteps receded, and with utmost care, Dominik set the bin back upright, wondering for a moment about the rows of chairs. He eased the door open. Hearing no new footsteps, he slipped into the hall and turned into the crossing hallway the men had come from. It was long, a mix of black and gray cabinets built into the walls, and lit only by sunlight filtering through the windows in each room's door. He headed toward the front of the building. His boots continued to squeak softly against the pristinely smooth floor. Not good. To compensate, he stopped sneaking and focused on walking as if he belonged there. A furtive tread would alert the guards.

Where *were* the guards?

He passed a half-dozen classrooms on both sides of the hall before he heard voices around another corner. They weren't approaching, but seemed to be engaged in a worried conference. He stopped at the bend and cocked his head, listening. At least four voices, a mix of male and female, their tones tense as they spoke over each other too fast for him to follow. He couldn't discern more than individual words. Words like "hell" and "damned" were spoken as curses as much as descriptors. Clearly, the rough speech of the Devil's servants.

A door opened in that unseen hallway, and a voice Dominik recognized spoke over the others. It was the large nobleman from the one-sided fight back at the farm, and the voices quieted. He roared, "Coming through!" before the babble rose again. New voices joined in, and Dominik heard a woman address Rebecca by name.

Rebecca!

"We don't (something unintelligible) in Grantville," the woman said with a tone that implied finality.

Dominik wished he understood more English, but at least now he had a name for this Devil's town. Grantville.

The noise of the crowd seemed to be moving away, so he risked a glance around the corner. They were departing, headed toward a set of glass doors—such perfect glass!—at the end of the hall. At least two of the men still carried those sleek firearms. In their midst, he recognized Rebecca's cap and curly black hair. Her eyes wide and fearful, she was speaking with a middle-aged woman.

Then a break in the departing crowd showed something that nearly stopped Dominik's heart. Herr Abrabanel was being carried out on a stretcher. He looked weak. His hand reached for Rebecca's, but she was too far away.

What had they done to him? What were they *going* to do to him?

The crowd pushed through the glass doors and disappeared. Dominik scrambled across the hallway to a room that should look out onto the front courtyard. He was careful to close the door behind him before he half-crawled, half-ran to the low windows lining the far wall. Raising just his eyes above the sill, he scanned the courtyard.

Two of the strange coaches moved without horses, growling as if they were alive and hungry. He couldn't see inside the lead vehicle, a large boxy thing, but the second one held Rebecca and the nobleman. The coaches navigated around their fellows in the courtyard before accelerating with matching roars. They turned onto the road and disappeared behind the trees.

Dominik slumped to the floor. His rescue had failed. The Abrabanels were gone.

* * *

He snuck out of the school and back into the forest, intent on waiting until darkness fell so he could at least steal his coach back. But what would he do then? Return to Amsterdam? It had been his home for two decades now. He and his young wife had moved there to start a new life away from their families' farms. After she died, he'd seen no reason to return to Germany. But returning home would mean abandoning the Abrabanels. Yet how could he find them? Where would he even start?

Back at his original vantage point, Dominik lay down to watch and wait, to try to discern more about these people. He rested his chin on the backs of his hands, aware of how bone-deep weary he was. It had been a long day. It was good to rest. Good to...

Dominik awoke with a start. He was cold, alone, and in nearly complete darkness. Dim moonlight filtered through the trees, and nighttime sounds filled the air: chirps and rustles and the abrupt cry of something small dying. It was that cry that woke him.

His gaze snapped to the school. The courtyard was empty, and there were no signs of life. Dominik's breath hitched. His coach and team were gone. Everyone was gone.

"Some rescuer you are," he muttered as he rose, cursing himself and his tired, aching body. Unsure what else to do, he turned and walked through the woods, following the dark snake of the road, headed in the same direction that the locals had taken the Abrabanels. He would have made better time walking on the road, but he didn't want to risk meeting one of those accursed coaches. The dark lay heavy on Dominik's soul, spiraling his thoughts downward.

After a time, he mentally kicked himself for wallowing in self-pity. The Abrabanels still needed him. He was frightened by the implications of this God-forsaken Grantville, but he *would* rescue them. Somehow. They were good people who didn't deserve to suffer at the hands of witches.

He didn't know how long he walked, stumbling over undergrowth and fallen logs in the dim moonlight. He passed dark buildings, skirted some fields, and crossed over a creek, but it felt like an eternity before he found a collection of buildings that he assumed were the outskirts of Grantville. They straddled the road, leaving no easy way around.

He hid behind a tree and gazed out. This cluster of houses wasn't nearly enough to support the massive school. One two-story building was lit as if they'd caged the sun itself within four walls and a roof. A sound similar to the growl of those horseless coaches came from behind the house. Despite the obvious and casual use of magic, Dominik was intrigued. How did these people do that?

Exhausted curiosity brought him onto the road. He neared the lit house and stepped onto neatly cropped grass. He would just peek through a window. It boggled his mind to realize that every building he saw had such perfect, large-paned windows. But, perhaps, he could see something useful through one, something to help him find—

A dog's bark split the night like Cerberus himself was coming for Dominik's soul. He jumped back with a yell and fell onto something small and hard. The object squeaked once, high and sharp and loud. The dog, no bigger than a young boar and just as solid, leapt from the shadows around the edge of the building and charged across the lawn, barking its intent to tear Dominik to shreds.

Dominik scrambled back. He grabbed what he'd fallen on and flung it at the charging beast as he struggled to his feet. His throw went high and wide, but the dog changed directions mid-stride and leapt to snatch the object out of the air. The beast landed solidly, front legs splayed wide to hold its squat body. It growled and chomped the thing it had caught, releasing high-pitched squeaks like the cries of a dying squirrel. It wasn't a squirrel; it had felt smooth and vaguely squishy, like a stick that was rotten on the inside. The dog chomped it like a wurst. The squeaky cacophony only added to Dominik's already pounding terror.

He bolted down the road for the woods, only half-noticing when the dog stopped at the edge of the road. He sent a prayer of thanks for whatever had stayed the beast. He certainly couldn't have outrun it in the dark. Probably not in daylight either.

Dominik collapsed against a tree, breathing hard. Finding the Abrabanels was not going to be easy.

* * *

That was the longest night of Dominik's forty years. He stumbled through the forest, circling the town. At some point in the night, the entire town abruptly lit up as though the Devil's minions had all simultaneously unveiled a hundred miniature suns. Dogs barked, and Dominik heard a few raucous cheers. Bright, steady light streamed out of the windows and beamed down from high, arched street lamps. Dominik had never seen a lantern burn so bright or so steady as those lamps. The power of those impossible lights made the darkness feel that much more oppressive.

He moved furtively through the forest, like a deer wary of the hunter. Several times, he forded streams that seemed to crisscross the town and paused for a drink. Those were the only rests he granted himself. Near dawn, exhaustion finally pulled him into a thicket. He barely managed to crawl deep under the branches before sleep took him.

Three days Dominik repeated this pattern. He slept during the day and then explored Grantville's edges at night. In the deepest hours of darkness, he ventured onto the streets. He avoided the streets lit by those high, steadily glowing lamps. The Devil may work in darkness, but for now, so did Dominik. Even so, he was still chased away by no fewer than seven guard dogs. Some were contained by fences, others by nothing more than whatever compulsion or training kept them on their assigned lands. Grantville's citizens were very protective of their property to have such fierce guard dogs.

One dog wasn't stopped by the borders of its domain. It was a short thing that looked like a baguette with stubby legs. It slipped under its fence, yapping and snarling like an imp from hell itself. Dominik had never seen a dog like that before, and he prayed to God that he never would again. The thing sounded rabid as it chased him halfway back to the edge of town.

* * *

Gnawing hunger woke Dominik in mid-afternoon on the fourth day. He'd never been a wealthy man, but he'd moved to Amsterdam before the deprivations of war made hunger a constant companion for his fellow Germans. Starvation was not a tribulation he'd ever faced. Now, he lay on the reverse slope of a hill outside of Grantville, staring at the sky, hand on his empty belly. Was this how he would die?

His stomach gurgled.

He had to do something. He couldn't simply continue on like this, watching, waiting, stumbling through the dark. Starving. The Abrabanels needed him, but what could he do?

He'd run into a family of refugees from the war-ravaged countryside last night. A hollow-eyed mother and two bony children. Once she'd overcome her fear, once he'd convinced her that he too was a refugee, she'd confirmed something Dominik had come to suspect. She knew nothing more of this town than he did.

Grantville hadn't been here last week. The Devil's handiwork indeed. What if these strangers disappeared as quickly as they'd come? Would he ever find Herr Abrabanel and his daughter?

Dominik drew another deep breath and sat up. Leaves rustled overhead as sleep faded from his mind. He let the cheerful cacophony of birds wash over him, too weary to do more than worry.

A woman's delighted laugh wrenched Dominik from his melancholy. His eyes widened in surprise.

Rebecca and the tall nobleman were walking down the road, arm in arm, not twenty yards away. They'd passed him already and were walking toward town.

Dominik's fingers clutched at the forest's leafy mulch, squishing it between his fingers. "Finally," he said, relief washing over him. He'd found her! He wished he were a brave man, that he possessed the courage to rush out and rescue Rebecca. But memories of the nobleman's skill as a warrior put stop to any violent thoughts. Bravery was not an option. Stealth and patience were all he had.

At least they were treating Rebecca with courtesy. She looked well and healthy. Definitely better fed than Dominik was. It was more than he'd expected of her captors.

Rebecca and the nobleman strolled along, deep in conversation, paying no attention to their surroundings. Dominik wasn't surprised. Rebecca was quite the captivating conversationalist, always giving her full attention and demanding no less from those with her.

Dominik glanced up and down the road. Nobody else was in sight. This was his chance. As the two disappeared from view around a slight curve of the road, Dominik dashed through the woods paralleling it. His heart pounded in his chest, but he didn't stop. Couldn't stop. He couldn't lose Rebecca again.

The forest grew right up to the edge of the nearest house, a small, decrepit thing compared to its neighbors. The unfenced yard was so overgrown that it seemed the forest was slowly reclaiming the land. Dominik pressed himself against the wall and peered around the corner. They were still in view. After two pounding heartbeats, Dominik ran around the rear of the house and into the open. The next yard was better maintained, and the house was lined on one side with overgrown bushes. Dominik slithered into the space between bush and house and dropped to the ground. He peeked out at the street from a dog's-eye view of the world.

There they were, several houses down, strolling as though without a care in the world.

An intrusive thought pointed out that Rebecca was not acting like a captive. She seemed relaxed and was clearly enjoying the conversation. He pushed the thought aside.

A dog barked deep and loud from the other side of Dominik's wall. He jumped. Someone yelled at the dog but it continued barking and the door opened.

Time to move.

Dominik scrambled from his hiding place and bolted around the back to the next house. It had a wooden fence with alternating slats that would stop a dog but provided excellent footholds. He didn't even pause. He'd never been an athletic man, but he did *not* want to meet the beast behind that bark. Dominik dove over the fence, tumbled onto the grass, and came up running. Thank God the yard was empty. At the property's far side, feeling vulnerable and exposed, Dominik huddled behind the slatted fence and peeked over.

Several houses ahead, Rebecca and the nobleman continued along. The man laughed heartily at something Rebecca said.

Dominik followed them for three blocks as he darted and dashed, hid and peeked. Twice, he had to backtrack when someone was outside their house, and once he had to skirt entirely around a fenced property with three of those small, viciously yapping dogs, but he always found his quarry again. A hint of hope began to build in Dominik's chest.

He was going to find where they were holding Herr Abrabanel.

The couple turned right and disappeared briefly from view behind a house. Dominik was huddled fifty yards from the road they'd turned onto. He held his breath until they reappeared behind the house. The road was straight ahead of his position, giving him a clear view as they turned directly toward him. They disappeared into the second house on the street ahead of him and didn't reappear. A door slammed. Dominik grinned. He'd found the house.

It was unremarkable compared to its neighbors, white with brown trim, a yard that was perhaps a trifle better maintained, and only a low metal fence made of intertwined wire around the back yard. Why would they keep the Abrabanels here? According to the stories, noble prisoners held for ransom were often granted freedom within the grounds of their captor's castle. But simply placing them in an unprotected house near, not even inside, an unwalled town seemed...wrong.

Were they keeping Herr Abrabanel captive through witchcraft? Or were his injuries so severe that nobody worried about him escaping such a simple prison? Dominik nodded. Yes, that had to be it. Balthazar's injury would also tether Rebecca. Despite her relative freedom, she wouldn't escape without her father.

Dominik prayed that his assistance would be sufficient to help them both escape.

A rebellious corner of his mind noted that the house looked quite charming, nothing like he would have expected from practitioners of the dark arts. He could almost picture himself in such a house if he'd been a successful merchant.

He pushed the thought roughly aside. The Devil was cunning in his temptations.

Dominik worried about their escape. He hadn't found his coach and team and had no idea how to operate one of those horseless coaches. They would have to run back up the road, Dominik and Rebecca supporting the injured Herr Abrabanel...a plan dependent on nobody realizing they'd escaped. If they could reach the woods, they'd be free.

Dominik ghosted through the remaining space to the back of the house. He paused at each hiding space, watching and waiting. Every movement was calculated to minimize his exposure as he neared the house. He leapt the low metal fence and dashed to press himself against the white house's rear wall. The spindly bush he hid behind wasn't large enough to completely hide him, but he should be unnoticeable to the casual observer. The bush's purple flowers gave off a heady perfume as if in counterpoint to Dominik's stench. Four days of sleeping in the dirt hadn't done him any favors.

The front door slammed again, and Dominik peered cautiously around the corner. He didn't see anything at first, but then the broad-shouldered nobleman passed into view, walking swiftly back the way he'd come. Alone.

Dominik pulled back and breathed deeply, trying and failing to calm his nerves. The Abrabanels were inside. He edged to the window beside the back door and peered in through the bottom corner. The kitchen he saw was well-appointed with fine furniture. Wood-paneled cupboards sat above neat counters. A small table sat under the window. Dominik nearly jumped when he realized that someone was sitting at that table, no more than one foot away. It was the middle-aged woman who'd been talking to Rebecca back at the school. She was sipping from a mug, talking with someone out of view. Dominik couldn't make out her words through the glass, but that didn't matter. He wasn't sneaking in through the back.

He squatted down and considered. He saw no easy way to reach the second-story window, and the side windows he'd glimpsed looked too high for easy access.

That left the front door.

Dominik steeled himself and slipped around the house. The land descended enough so that the wooden stairs out front were more than he'd expected. He crept up them, careful to place his feet along the edges to minimize squeaking. He paused at the edge of the covered front porch. Several windows showed a parlor with plush furniture, but no people that he could see. He prayed that the door was unlocked.

In one smooth motion, Dominik crossed the porch, opened the door, and slid inside. Striving for silence, he kept the handle pressed down and closed the door with the barest *click*.

Apparently, that was enough.

"Morris?" the woman called from the kitchen. "You're back early."

Carpeted stairs climbed upward to Dominik's right. His pulse pounded in his ears, and everything screamed at him to run, but he forced himself to walk steadily up the stairs as though he lived there. As he'd done all those years ago when infiltrating the bakery, *der Brezelgeist* again carefully placed his feet near the edges of the treads, praying they wouldn't squeak.

They did. But he kept his steps purposeful and plodding. No hurry, no need for anyone to worry. He belonged here.

Small portraits lined the stairs, eerily lifelike paintings of young and old, and not all of them in the traditional portraiture pose. Children smiled at him from those pictures. That argumentative corner of Dominik's mind mused, "Even the Devil's own have families. They look happy." The top of the stairs ended in two doors, the ceiling slanting with the angle of the roof. Dominik took a chance and tried the door to the right. It held Herr Abrabanel.

Balthazar was sitting up in a bed beside the door, reading a book. His face was pale under his dark hair, but his eyes were alert. He looked up when Dominik slipped inside. His eyes widened.

"Dominik?" Quiet astonishment filled the doctor's face. "I thought you'd run away."

Shame filled Dominik's throat and froze him in place. "I...I'm sorry I abandoned you." He knelt and clutched Herr Abrabanel's hand. "I would beg your forgiveness, but we have no time if we wish to escape. Can you walk with your injuries?"

Herr Abrabanel set his book down. "Slow down, my friend. I am not injured. And why would I need to escape?"

Dominik's mouth bobbed open as his mind stutter-stepped. "But I saw you on the stretcher. I don't know what the large nobleman did to you—"

"Who?"

"The man with the broad shoulders who led the butchery of Tilly's mercenaries."

"Ah, that would be Michael. He didn't injure me. He saved me." Herr Abrabanel tapped his chest. "My heart failed. I would have died if he and Doctor Nichols hadn't been there."

Dominik's brows pinched as his thoughts swirled. That calm, annoying part of his mind put the pieces together and spoke before his conscious mind caught up. "They rescued you. You're not a prisoner awaiting ransom...you're a guest." His mouth clicked shut as he reassembled what he knew in this new light.

Herr Abrabanel nodded.

"But they practice witchcraft!" Dominik blurted. "How can you sit here so calmly amidst the very evidence of their evil? Their horseless coaches and captured sunlight. No oil lamp ever burned that steadily!" He pointed toward the slanted ceiling, at the bubble of glass that shone pure white light about the room. "Even those perfect portraits on the stairs that no artist ever painted—witchcraft is the only explanation for all of this!"

Herr Abrabanel's laugh was warm and soft. He patted Dominik's hand that clutched his own and said, "There is another explanation, one more wonderful and mysterious than anyone could imagine. I truly believe that we have been witness to a miracle." The old man's calm eyes transfixed Dominik. "Let me tell you about the Ring of Fire."

* * *

Half an hour later, Dominik sat on a small chair in the corner of Herr Abrabanel's room, shaking his head in wonder. Rebecca sat on the end of the bed—she and the woman who lived here had come to check on their patient after Dominik's not-quite-stealthy-enough entrance—her happy smile confirming the bizarre tale. An entire town transported through both space and time? These strangers were from a version of the Americas over three hundred years in the future? Crazy!

But he couldn't deny the evidence before him. With everything he'd seen, it was an answer that made sense. Especially if he could accept Herr Abrabanel's assertion that these were not Devil-worshiping witches. The violence he'd seen at the farmhouse had been the men of Grantville fighting to save the farmer and his wife from Tilly's men, not butchers reveling in their butchery. And they had saved them. Both were recovering well. These "Americans" had acted with honor. More honor, certainly, than Dominik had shown when he ran away.

Herr Abrabanel waited in silence while Dominik processed everything he'd been told. Finally, the old man asked, "So, you truly infiltrated both the school and Grantville itself without being noticed?"

Dominik nodded.

"That is...impressive." The old man's expression turned thoughtful before he said, "I could use someone like you. Michael and the residents of Grantville are good people, but they face grave dangers in the days ahead. War surrounds them on all sides. I have decided to help, providing what information I can to assist them. The Abrabanel family has an extensive network of contacts in the region, but communication has been...problematic lately."

Rebecca snorted, a very unladylike sound. "More like nonexistent."

Her father nodded in agreement, then said, "I'd like to change that. I *need* to change that because accurate and timely information is vital to any undertaking, especially to war." He cleared his throat. "Let me be blunt, Dominik. I want you to be my spy, my eyes and ears in the region, serving in the guise of a courier. I have an associate I'd like to connect you with, a man skilled in the arts of spycraft, who could train you, if you're interested."

A spy? Dominik blinked silently. He'd never wanted to be anything more than a simple coachman.

"You could go back to Amsterdam," Herr Abrabanel said, sensing his reticence. "Your coach and team will be returned to you regardless, but I truly believe that you could make a difference in the lives of these people. They're good people, Dominik. A bit rough around the edges, perhaps, but God-fearing and honest. With our help, with *your* help, they can build a new home here. A safe haven in the midst of war."

"Why would you trust me again?" Dominik said. "I abandoned you. You could have died!"

"God forgives us. Who am I to do any less?"

The sudden lump in Dominik's throat precluded any response.

"Besides," Herr Abrabanel continued, "if we hadn't met the Americans, I *would* have died." He smiled that warm smile, then lay back. The conversation was clearly tiring him. "God works in mysterious ways."

Dominik hung his head, and days of spring-tight tension melted into tears that he couldn't hold back. He hadn't realized how badly he had needed Herr Abrabanel's forgiveness. "Thank you," he said quietly once he'd regained a semblance of control. He swiped at his eyes, and then he shook his head. "I am not a brave man. I don't know how—"

"Rubbish," Rebecca interrupted sharply. "Bravery is not the absence of fear. It's acting *despite* the fear. You infiltrated a village of supposed witches to save us. You thought Grantville was the Devil's own playground, and yet you came anyway. *That* is the kind of courage that breeds legends."

Dominik nodded, accepting her admonishment, though he wasn't sure about the last part. Their trust in him, despite everything that had happened, was a balm upon his soul. Now, Dominik couldn't imagine running back to Amsterdam to be just a coach driver. He wanted more. He wanted to help the Abrabanels and the strange people who'd saved them.

He wanted to prove that he was worthy of Balthazar Abrabanel's forgiveness.

Dominik would never consider himself a brave man, but he knew now that he could do what needed to be done. He squared his shoulders.

"I accept your offer," he said resolutely. "I will be your spy. You may call me '*der Brezelgeist.*'"

By Virginia DeMarce

The Arabian Queen
Virginia DeMarce

This story begins right after "The Play's The Thing" in Issue 11.

Butzbach, Province of the Main
April 1637

"Are you going to start mining *The Black Rose* pretty soon, Master Massinger?" Dick asked.

"You really should," Tom urged. "We can get another 'noble evil; common man good' play by re-working just a little bit of the story."

"Which part?"

"The legend that the hero and heroine were the parents of Thomas à Becket."

"But that's not true," Anna Maria protested.

"When has that ever had anything to do with our scripts?"

"I'm too busy," Massinger said. "Yes, the book has a lot of potential; I'm glad we have it. Right now, though, I'm working on something else. An alternate history of England; one in which Edward VI lived and neither Mary nor Elizabeth ever ascended the throne."

Tom looked up. "Let me have the Becket project, then, if the group likes the idea. I can work in some applicability to the way that Charles I has treated Archbishop Laud. Becket was an Archbishop of Canterbury and Laud is too. With some reference to strict English censorship." He narrowed his eyes. "With some kind of a joke on 'but would it play in Peoria?' And the other person answers, 'Maybe, but definitely not in London.' We can probably get away with that; even the Episcopalians in Grantville don't like Charles I."

"A lot of them aren't exactly crazy about Laud, either. Ever since he gave them Tom Simpson for a bishop."

"That appointment," Christina proclaimed, "is not going to come up in a Becket play. If you write a Becket play, that is not going to be mentioned. Not once. Not even in a sly aside."

"Would the dramatization of the Becket story impact the establishment of constitutional monarchy in the USE? And where is 'common man good' coming from?"

"Becket's family wasn't noble; his father was a merchant."

"Would it impact the controversies in the USE over an established church, or not, and how, and where? On the proper role of the clergy? I mean, 'Becket was a commoner' is good for a hero, but 'Becket thought the church could get away with defying the king' isn't likely to enthuse Gustav Adolf if we manage to play Magdeburg again."

"Maybe connect the 'commoner' theme to the expedition they're getting together to prevent slave societies from developing in North America? Have the king despise Becket partly because his mother was black, since *The Black Rose* says that Maryam was...exactly what *was* she?"

"Walter found her in Cathay? Maybe? There are so many places in that book that I can't keep them straight. But I don't think that the Anti-Slavery League folks would think that a girl from Cathay, or India, or Arabia, or even Egypt, was black. When they talk about black, they mean people from Africa. Not even from Egypt or Morocco. From the central part of the continent. From the places that the slaves who were taken to the New World come from. Most of them, at least."

"But we've just got to do a Becket play, now that it's come up. Some of the dialogue is just too good to pass by. What, exactly, did the king say that his men interpreted to mean that he wanted Becket killed? Did the king mean to say that, or was he just blowing off steam?"

"Hey, if you go that way, we could have a steam engine on the stage for special effects!"

"Wolf!" Christina shrieked.

"There are several versions. I think the shortest one is, 'Will no one rid me of this turbulent priest?' but the contemporary biography made His Majesty a lot more eloquent: 'What miserable drones and traitors have I nourished and brought up in my household, who let their lord be treated with such shameful contempt by a low-born cleric?'" Tom laughed. "That's really pretty eloquent; I don't think I could do better if I made it up myself."

"The 'knights' could be turned into *Reichsritter*. That wouldn't be much of a problem."

That turned into one more new play in the bank.

* * *

"The more I think about it," Massinger said, "the more certain I become that the company can make *The Black Rose* the basis for several plays." He held up the very substantial tome that was under discussion—again. Tom kept bringing it up, insisting that since they had it, they should be using it.

"After all, Costain himself divided it into three books."

Christina frowned. "There's no possible way that any play will have time to show the whole journey to Cathay with everything that went on. Not unless it lasts for ten hours. And that's only part of Book One."

"Not unless it's a trilogy," Dick said.

Christina snorted. "Quadrilogy? Quintilogy? Sextology?"

"Perhaps each of the three 'books' in the 'book as a whole' could provide more than one, ah..."

"Source of inspiration."

Dick made an imaginary note on an imaginary clipboard. "Wonderful. Make a note of that for use on the posters once it gets that far. 'Inspired by' sounds so much better than 'plagiarized from,' don't you think?"

"I'm filing a formal protest against that, brother mine." Tom said. "It's not really plagiarism when a fellow has to turn all that prose description into blank verse dialogue accompanied by stage directions. Give the dramatist some credit, here!"

* * *

Valentin Wagner thought that they should do *The Taming of the Shrew* next. Mostly because he wanted to be one of Bianca's suitors. If Margarethe Lehr was Bianca.

"We could, I suppose." Dick looked around the *Landgrafenschloss*, taking potential cast members into account. "Ludovic does a really good job with Petruchio. Christina already knows Katharina. I'm not going to put an amateur in as Bianca, though, when Anna Maria already knows the role. For the other suitors..." There were a couple of unfamiliar faces around. "Who's that?"

"Horst?"

"Is that his given name? Never heard that one."

"No. Family name. Johann Daniel Horstius, to Latinize it, as he has done. He's studying medicine, has been to Leahy in Grantville, and is enrolled at Jena. He comes back every now and then in hopes of keeping dibs on Elisabeth until he can afford to get married. Which will probably not be for another ten years."

Elisabeth was Elisabeth Schupp, sister of "the guy who's teaching at the normal school in Amberg" and one of the "kids" from Giessen who were providing extras for the cast while learning what they could about up-timers.

"She's not old enough to get married, either."

"Which works out well. Waiting ten years will be fine for her."

At one end of the room, Zach Schaupp and Johannes Schupp were trying to figure out whether they might be related. When it became clear that Zach and Wolfgang's folks were from Saxe-Weimar, the chaperoning Frau Schupp decided that they were probably not. Somewhat to her relief.

Horst was indulging himself in major criticism of Lord Philipp's present court physician, citing his incompetence in the matter of the margrave's heart attack. The physician came to his own defense. The result might have been described as controversy.

"When Mögling stalked out in a huff," Jim wrote to Lorrie, "Horst transferred his all-knowing general *Besserwisser*-ness to proclaiming that apprenticeships are old-fashioned, and telling Zach that when the Butzbach stint is over, Wolfgang needs to go back to school. Mike tried to shut him up by saying that you think so, too. Then Wolf threatened to run away if anybody tries to make him. I think he meant it."

They did *The Taming of the Shrew*, adding in a few songs from the up-time version so that Ludovic's talent with the lute should not be wasted.

* * *

Massinger delegated to Tom the job of sorting out the several potential plots that might be found in *The Black Rose* and went back to *Edward VI*, an alternate history in which Mary Tudor was married off early to Alberto, a fictional royal Spanish younger son. Although widowed comparatively young, the king appointed her as his regent in the Kingdom of Naples. Although sadly childless (thus avoiding the problem of part-Spanish potential claimants to the English throne), Mary lived as long and happily and effectively ever after as had Archduchess Isabella Clara Eugenia in the Netherlands. *The Vicereine of Napolita*. Upon what magnificent diplomatic triumph should she end her career?

He pulled the sheets of paper together, lining up the edges neatly. If he could take it to Magdeburg...to a better venue than he could afford last fall...tempt Sophia Elisabeth of Brandenburg to return to them as the young Mary...

If he could only figure out what to do with Elizabeth, who was unwilling to be disposed of so easily...not to mention the Scottish Mary.

Who maybe deserved a play of her own. A tragedy. What was the song about Mary Hamilton? He had heard it in Grantville. One of the vinyl recordings that Mistress Mundell had...a singer with a Spanish name...four Marys.

What could drive a young woman to commit the act of infanticide when the child was royal and, apparently, its paternity was known and acknowledged, "from the kitchens up to the hall"? A mental disorder? A previous religious vow that she had broken by the affair? But if she carried the child to term in order not to kill it through her own self-murder, why do so after the birth? The most important tie would be from this Mary to the queen; not to the king.

Ah, her French husband did not die young. Mary Queen of Scots is the faithful wife of a philandering husband, to whom she has dutifully borne the heirs he needs while enduring the endless insults of a wicked Italian mother-in-law and royal mistresses far more beautiful than she. The king values her only because of the unlikely inheritance claims those heirs may someday bring to bear against her English cousins. She bears with dignity that he has never, from the first instant of their marriage, pretended to respect his marriage vows. She *can* bear it as long as she does have loyalty from her childhood friends, her life-long ladies-in-waiting, the companions who will never betray her. So the focus of Mary Hamilton's guilt...Mary was not forced...No—she succumbed to *real* temptation, went *willingly* to the bed of the handsome and charismatic king...

He should sleep now. Probably eat something. He looked around. How did it get to be so late? The marvelous mantel lantern that let a man come close to turning night into day, even without the miracle of up-time electricity, needed to be refilled. If only the fuel smelled better...

Massinger's fingers twitched. He reached for another sheet of paper.

* * *

Tom sat up and ran his fingers through his hair. "What's equivalent to Saxons and Normans these days?"

"Just use Saxons and Normans," Wolfgang suggested. "Making sure that the Saxons are the good guys, because they were Germans. Normans were French, so that's good to go as bad guys, given the machinations of Monsieur Gaston."

"Is that a good idea?" Jim Mundell shook his head. "You know, John George of Saxony and all that."

"They were different Saxons," Mike argued.

"Thuringians?" Wolf suggested.

Suggestions buzzed around and around the breakfast table.

"You can't make it up-timers vs. down-timers. Remember *Franconia!* The farmers and the ranchers have to be friends these days."

"Set the scene where the story begins in Hungary. I'm sure that there must be at least one university in Hungary. The Magyars can be the good guys and the Ottomans the foreign oppressors."

"Or Italy. Italy always works as a spot to drop a play. Noble native Italians oppressed by Spanish occupation forces."

"Stick with England!"

"Oh, all right. But I'll make the Saxons into Danes, just to be safe. This will be a Massinger play, after all, not a Quiney play. Walter of Gurnie can be a Dane."

"Are there Danes named Walter?"

"There must be a few."

"Are you sure that's safe? Absolutely sure?"

"Why not?"

"Christian IV of Denmark has a whole bunch of illegitimate sons. A couple of them, at least. Plus Waldemar, who's sort of half-and-half."

"Denmark's fair game. Grandpa used it for Hamlet, so we have squatter's rights. In a pinch, we can say he's a Scot living in Denmark. I've met several Scots named Walter. You run into Scots anywhere you go."

"That should do it. Forget England!"

"How about the illegitimate son of a Scots laird, now living in Denmark?"

"Hah! That should really do it." Jim grinned. "Not to reference anyone in particular who might have wandered into Grantville once upon a time." They all smirked a bit.

* * *

"Do we need Engaine?"

"She'd make a better play on her own with her as the central character. Her mother-in-law as the second."

"Do we have an actress who's up to either of them?"

"Not here. Not even in Grantville. But with a good enough play, we could attract a good enough actress."

"If Master Massinger should take us to Magdeburg again, in a better venue than we had last fall, perhaps we could tempt Sophia Elisabeth of Brandenburg to rejoin us for this role. There's no singing, but..."

"For her voice, we could find a composer to provide a...what are those called?"

"Leitmotif."

"I think we should separate the play with Engaine from any of the rest of this book."

"How so?"

"Give her some other hero; just make his name up. Change the date and place. In *The Tragedy of Engaine of Bulaire, Part 1*, use the 'Walter of Gurnie' circumstances from Costain's Book One, but change all the names; then just refer to 'after this, he goes off, has foreign adventures, etc.' In the last scene, she's married to his rich and legitimate half-brother and watching him ride away.

"Then for *The Tragedy of Engaine of Bulaire, Part 2*, skip over the whole middle part of *The Black Rose*; pick up when not-Walter comes home even richer than her husband, with a foreign wife, and how she reacts. Even if she *doesn't* have a moral leg to stand on because she married someone else first. Who needs witches when a couple of females like Engaine and the dowager countess of Bulaire are available? It's just frosting on the cake that the countess is Engaine's mother-in-law and the two of them conspire together instead of being at odds with each other. If you ask me, they're Costain's best inspiration in this book. The male villains are fairly trite, but these ladies are *wicked*."

"That's..." Tom stroked his chin. "That's a good idea, actually, and it gets rid of any need to have all that long prologue in the first play that focuses on Walter and Maryam."

"Prologue? There's no prologue?"

"As far as Maryam is concerned, almost all of Book One is a prologue. She doesn't show up in most of it. The 'Walter and Maryam' plot can just start when a pair of young European adventurers show up in Antioch and join an expedition to far Cathay to make their fortunes. As far as it needs an introduction, I'll work in a bit of backstory for her; not so much for him."

* * *

"Exactly when was that attack on Freiherr von Mitwitz's castle in Franconia?"

"In the summer of 1634," Christina said. "July, maybe—about then? Not so long ago. I know that you boys wouldn't report to Magdeburg that Lord Philipp had given sanctuary to the children of witch persecutors, but there's no way that Eila could know it. On the basis of everything she's been through, she was right to take those children out of the *Spital* and run."

"Maybe she was absolutely right to do it," Zach said, "not just relatively right. I honestly couldn't make anybody a guarantee that some of the guys in the CoCs wouldn't take things out on kids. Or on people who give sanctuary to the wrong kids, like the margravine said the mayor's wife was worried about. Or, for that matter, that anybody else might not take things out on another anybody who might be related to somebody who got on the wrong side of things."

* * *

"Don't bother me right now, Dick," Master Massinger said. He had ink on his fingers, his nose, his cuffs.

"But..."

"Can't you see that I'm writing?"

* * *

Dick flopped down next to Christina. "He's writing, all right. He's obsessed. He's writing several pages a day. But he won't even look at these outlines that he told Tom to work up for him. Or tell me what I should be doing next. I have no idea if Tom's outlines are even close to what he wants."

Her response was to sit straight up. "Whether he pays attention or not, we have to present three new—new, *brand* new—plays at the spring fair. That's in the contract he signed. Three that haven't been staged in public."

Tom waved his pen at the rest of them. "I'll keep outlining so they'll be ready to go the instant we get his attention back. Maybe stick in some stage directions. Bits of dialogue here and there. That will give the actors a head start. So...where were we?"

Ludovic snagged the last piece of salt pork. "We were planning on writing a large, juicy, part for Ludovic Gaines?"

Anna Maria threw her spork at him. "Nitwit. You have oatmeal where you should have brain matter. When you shake your head, it sloshes around. You are more unduly pleased with yourself than... What? Words, I need more words."

Anna Maria, in her scanty spare time, was experimenting with writing a play. If Tom could do it, why couldn't she? If the great-grandson of a glove-maker from a provincial town like Stratford-upon-Avon in provincial England could write plays, why not the daughter of a successful perfumer from less-provincial Villach in less-provincial Carinthia?

She was no ex-chambermaid like Christina. No penniless refugee who had come to Grantville for sanctuary in a war-torn world.

Mama and Papa were, perchance, just a bit...She sought the word. *Opportunistic*. Her parents had placed her with Shawna Masaniello in 1631 so she could go to school for a couple of years and then apprentice to what they regarded as a prestigious and well-paid job as a beautician. Two years ago, after the election that transferred the capital, they had left her younger brothers successfully placed at the Lothlorien Farbenwerke in Grantville and moved on to Bamberg, where they were doing well catering to the would-be elites of the State of Thuringia-Franconia.

She still needed more words, but she would have them. Her scanty traveling luggage included a reprint of *Roget's Thesaurus*, carefully wrapped in waterproof canvas to protect it from the elements.

* * *

"Maybe in *The Arabian Queen, Part 1*, you can do something topical with the student riot that Walter gets caught up in at the beginning. Maybe reference the one in Jena during the Rudolstadt Colloquy?"

Zach put up his hand as if he were in class. "The raid on the Countess of Bulaire's castle can reference the Ram Rebellion and the CoCs in Franconia."

Tom waved the clipboard. "Nope. Remember: That early stuff is going into the Engaine play...which Master Massinger isn't going to start writing yet, because he's busy with the Tudors. But we need to be pretty clear—sort out which episodes go into which play, or if they're going to be omitted entirely. This play starts when he gets to Antioch."

"Once he does get around to writing Engaine, he won't even need to reference the Ram Rebellion; when it's on stage, everybody will catch on," Wolfgang added.

"By the time he gets around to writing..." Dick's exasperation showed through in his voice. "If ever! I'm hoping that he won't even need to reference Costain's book for *The Arabian Queen*: just fill in the blanks in Tom's outlines."

"Which play is going to get all the technological advances from Cathay—papermaking, gunpowder, the telescope, and the compass. They can be from the up-timers," Jim Mundell said.

Dick shook his head. "That's so obvious that it's almost too obvious."

Jim persisted. "But does Engaine's ex-boyfriend bring them home in that play, or does Walter bring them home in this play?

"Why not both?" Anna Maria asked. "People aren't going to be watching both of them at the same time. Engaine's boyfriend can bring them from Cathay; Walter can bring them from the Mughals. That way, audiences can tell that they're seeing two different plays." She stood up. "Where's Ludovic this morning? If he spent the night chasing barmaids in Butzbach and came dragging in late, with a hangover...He's on stage first thing at rehearsal."

Mike got up. "I'll go look. Drag him downstairs for a bucket of cold water over his head, if I need to."

"This whole book needed a lot more Maryam and a lot less Walter, if you ask me," Wolfgang said. "It's always a good idea to have a beautiful heroine escape from a harem."

Wolf was beginning to develop an interest in girls—of a different type than just observing them for characteristics he could pick up when he was called to act a female role.

Christina achieved the Raised Eyebrow of Doom. "Believe me, when we put it on a stage, we aren't going to have eighty-one harem girls."

Dick grinned. "Not unless we can persuade the Jesuits to put it on as one of their huge spectacles."

"I don't think that they go in for harem girls." Tom stood up and tossed the clipboard to Christina. "I'll go with Mike. Jim, Zach, you come with us. We've most likely got a romantic hero to sober up."

They let the door slam behind them.

* * *

"Why an *Arabian* queen?"

The wine cellars kept a more even temperature than the upper floors at Philippseck. Cool, but not outright cold. They didn't need gloves. Dick had decided they might as well rehearse; they had gotten to the point of doing preliminary blocking with Tom's tentative stage directions, even if Master Massinger hadn't written any dialogue for them yet.

"Maryam isn't Arabian in the book. She's from India, isn't she?" Anna Maria persisted.

"Well, I don't want to use *Indian* queen," Tom waved vaguely toward the west. "With all the headlines about the expeditions to the New World, what the Dutch are doing, what the French are doing, what the USE is doing, and such, too many people would think that the play was about Pequots in New England or natives in the Caribbean or something."

"Not far Cathay," Ludovic said. He was starting to look a little better.

"Cathay isn't coming into this play, no matter the China expedition." Tom looked at the stage. "That isn't working; from the floor, the audience can't see Anna Maria because she's blocked behind Frau Keplerin. Change places, the two of you."

He took a look from stage right, then from stage left, then moved back for a better view. "The Mongol general is getting his own play. Right now, I'm thinking we should leave Walter and Maryam in India; the Mughals can substitute for the Chinese dowager empress without a long, tiresome journey that there's no way to show on a stage. Mughals have harems, I'm sure of it. And I can scarcely use *The African Queen*."

That led to a discussion of the movie, which Wolfgang and Zach had seen in Grantville. Which led to a discussion of Katharine Hepburn. Which led to a discussion of how to tell Katharine Hepburn from Audrey Hepburn.

"They're both terribly skinny," was Zach's contribution. "So thin that it pains you to look at them. You want to take them out and feed them dumplings."

In his evaluation of feminine pulchritude, Zach was very much a modern man. Modern, as in sharing the tastes of Pieter Paul Rubens. Deeply in favor of an abundance of opulent curves.

"Yeah," Ludovic said. "Oh, yeah." He was still feeling the pain, but he was onstage. "Actually, Christina's so brunette that she would make a fine Arabian queen."

* * *

"What are you going to do with the famous Mongol general if he's not involved with Walter and Maryam?"

"Bayan of the Hundred Eyes? I told you already that he'll be in a completely different play. We'll give him his own plot to be the hero of. His own heroine."

Tom thought for a minute. "A mature heroine. I want Master Massinger to play the general, because we'll need Ludovic for Tristan. Take a break."

Anna Maria plopped down on one of the empty beer kegs that on the rehearsal stage served for everything from cathedral altars (two, one piled on top of the other) to royal thrones (one for a seat with two stacked behind it to represent the back and canopy). There was a plentiful supply of them in the Philippseck wine cellars. "When Walter decides to go home, Tristan can change jobs...stay in Cathay..."

"India!" Tom screeched.

"There weren't any Mongols in India. You'll have to write that when Walter left to return to...wherever he's returning to...never-never-land... Tristan journeyed farther to the east and became Bayan's sidekick, which would sort of tie two plays together. There's already the scene where Tristan shows the longbow to the Mongol horde."

"Which, if you ask me," Mike Mundell said, "is sort of equivalent to one of the up-timers going off and showing their best technology to the Ottomans. At least from the perspective of the parts of Europe that the Mongols invaded. They were successful enough without it."

"Hey, a hero has to be physically heroic." Ludovic excelled at physical heroics.

"But Tristan isn't a hero; he's a sidekick."

"He could be the hero, if..." Ludovic coaxed.

"There's even what Renee Carson would call a 'big miss' with Maryam and Tristan and the language lessons. It's lucky they all had more sense than Othello and Desdemona."

"Yeah. It may get dicey at times, but *The Arabian Queen's* going to be a comedy rather than a tragedy. Not a 'ha-ha' comedy, but a 'happy ending' comedy. And all that stuff, negotiations and the like, that eventually gets him to the point of marrying her needs to be really condensed. Like two hundred or so pages into twenty minutes. Same for all the peace negotiations leading up to the 'politely imprisoned by the dowager empress' stage."

"Can we put something in there that would remind people about Melissa Mailey and Rita Stearns and the others being locked in the Tower of London?"

"Yeah." Tom scribbled a marginal note.

"Then we get to where Walter is becoming disgusted with the feudal system in England when he sees common men fighting for their rights in Cathay. That can be parlayed into an act in which he leads a revolution like the Ram Rebellion when he gets home."

"Hey, design it so that he deliberately goes home to use his wealth to lead a rebellion and Tristan doesn't agree with that project, so that's why he joins the Mongol general instead."

"Can do."

"Why does Maryam miss the boat? We have to have her wandering on foot, calling for Walter, but I keep asking myself why he didn't bother to teach her any English during the time that they were canoodling in the palace of the dowager empress. They were already married, so unless he was planning to abandon her, he must have known that it would be a big help if she learned some before they got back home to never-never-land."

"Not never-never-land. Denmark. I'll think of something."

Tom stood up. "Let me start all over again. *The Tragedy of Engaine of Bulaire* plays (*Part 1 and Part 2*), as yet untitled, which will be tragic, tragic, classically tragic, terribly tragic, tragedies; a Walter and Maryam play (*The Arabian Queen, Part 1*) that spends more time on Maryam; and a *Part 2* in which he becomes a successful rebel, and she finally rejoins him. Triumphal reunification, rewards from a benevolent monarch, and all that."

"How about the servant boy? Mahmoud somebody," Jim Mundell asked.

"*That's* who we can use to tie it all into the Anti-Slavery League." Tom scribbled a note into the margin. "Since he's with Maryam all the way on her quest. She can be helping him escape from a cruel owner."

"But he's already helping her escape from a wicked uncle."

"They're helping one another escape."

"What happened to the harem?"

"She escaped from that earlier."

"With *The Mongol General* somewhere off to the side. If Master Massinger decides it needs a friend, I can do an outline for *The Chinese Dowager* to make a pair, but I don't even have time to think about her right now."

Christina clapped her hands. "Break's over." She pursed her lips. "Gee, it *will* be a hexalogy. I thought I was joking."

* * *

"So Walter gets home and..." Anna Maria was listening to Tom's latest inspiration.

"It came to me overnight, in a dream. He's going home to lead a revolution."

"I thought we'd already established that."

"I'd only gotten to the point that there would be one, the way it is in the book. Not that he went home to do it on purpose, because he has received hints of a plot against the rightful king. I'll add that as soon as I get to my desk."

"And?"

"He's leading it against the Oxenstierna Plot. He'll reveal the nefarious actions of George of Hesse-Darmstadt, Friedrich of Hesse-Homburg, and the counts of the Wetterau in both Hesse and Berlin. They'll have to have different names, of course, since he's a Scot living in Denmark, but..."

Anna Maria perceived no problem, and she was the mature one: twenty years old to Tom's eighteen. Nor had she, any more than Tom, been present upon the occasion when Massinger mentioned something of the sort to their patron, who winced.

Neither had Massinger mentioned to his junior partners Lord Philipp's negative reaction to his suggestion of this idea, specifically because the youngsters would have made a big fuss and yelled about censorship and giving in to pressure and things like that. He had just sort of slid them into Richard III at the time.

"I could help you," she offered. "Make the clean copies or something."

* * *

Margravine Dorothea, who was more than a little cynical and skeptical, repeated to her husband that she really doubted the wisdom of the proposed reconciliation that Philipp, as dear and sweet a man as he was, was attempting. Indeed, she was concerned that by making the effort, he might find himself in some difficulty with the imperial government.

Christian Wilhelm, who was indeed not in the least dumb, even if terminally indolent, gradually leaked to Tom Quiney more and more of the specific gossip that he had collected over the past year and a half concerning precisely what went on behind the scenes in Berlin, including what was done by whom, who did what with whom, and with what intent. Also, most usefully from the perspective of a young man who was writing a play, who said precisely what to whom, where, when, and why.

* * *

"*Schloss* Philippseck, Münster (not the one in Westphalia), bei Butzbach

"Tuesday

"Dear Mom,

"They fed us smoked, dried herring for breakfast. I can eat almost anything, but honest to God! Mom, that's just a bit much at just-barely-sunrise-o'clock. I choked it down, but Mike turned green and headed for the latrines.

"We've been spending quite a bit of time down at the *Landgrafenschloss* in town, since there are fewer of us to go there than there are miscellaneous play-volunteers from the town who would have to come up here. Last count, we had on stage for *Love's Labour's Lost* two *Keplerinnen*, two schoolteacher's daughters, three wives of various Butzbach city councilmen (with kids), one resident artist (Wagner isn't bad at this, which is more than I can really say for most of the rest—he took the role of the king of Navarre), and probably a partridge in a pear tree.

"One of the schoolteacher's daughters put on pants (the modern puffy kind; Christina wouldn't let her wear tights) and did a totally hilarious riff on her own dad as Holofernes the schoolmaster. That's why we put so many kids on stage, and it was worth it. Her sister played Jacquenetta. Ludovic was hilarious as Don Adriano, and Wolf played Moth.

"Apparently, the Butzbachers think it's a good idea to get their kids in front of Lord Philipp at some time before they'll really be in need of his patronage and wanting letters of recommendation for getting into schools or apprenticeships or whatever they're planning to do.

"I think Lord Philipp is getting restive because of too many plays by Massinger and Marlowe and Shakespeare and other English dramatists that he's already seen several times before. We're going to have to throw more new plays into the mix, but one a week makes a hectic schedule.

"Love you always,

"Jim"

* * *

"Do you suppose we could get Attacus Williams' wife to play Maryam if we put it on in Grantville?" Wolfgang asked. "She's a Gypsy; she probably looks more like an Arabian than anyone else for a hundred miles in any direction."

"Except for the rest of her family." Zach was a pragmatic sort of fellow.

"If Master Massinger puts this on in Grantville, maybe they'd be extras for the scenes set in India." Ludovic contributed. "It would save on stage make-up and Christina's always yelling about the expense."

"Why is Maryam Arabian in the play, anyway?" Wolf frowned. "The book says she was from India, doesn't it?"

"No, she's not from India," Christina said. "That's just where Walter ran into her. At least, I think that's where he ran into her. Except that Antioch is in Turkey: I remember that from catechism class. Sometimes I suspect that Costain wanted to write a travel guidebook more than he wanted to write a novel. So many places...If we had a computer, we could put all this in a spreadsheet."

"If wishes were horses, then beggars would fly. Most of the up-time computers that could display spreadsheets are dead or dying. I can't quite see us trying to travel with an aqualator."

"She's Arabian because I said so." That was Tom.

Everybody else ignored him.

"Can she act? Valeria Syracuse? Attacus' wife?" Anna Maria asked. "I've never met her."

"If she can't, she can just stand in the middle of the stage and wail for her husband, while other people act around her." That was Zach again.

"If she's not having another baby," Christina pointed out. "She already has one, I think."

"Maryam has a kid in the book; there must be some point where she was expecting it." Wolf grinned. "The stork doesn't really deliver them."

"Wasn't Sumitra Patel actually from India?" Jim asked.

"The exchange student?"

"Yeah," Mike said, "she was, but she moved to Bamberg to go to college. I have no idea where she is now. She was probably five years older than I am. Enough older that we never even talked to one another."

"Somebody at the high school ought to know," Jim said. "Maybe she'd come back."

"Not for one play, I don't think. Was she even *in* drama?"

"I hate to tell you guys, but I read the whole book again. Maryam was the sister of Anthemus, who was the merchant, who was *Greek*." Anna Maria twirled around. "Which means that Maryam was *Greek*. And she had blue eyes, which made Walter decide that she was half-*English*. She wasn't anything exotic at all, honestly. Definitely not Arabian. Maryam was just nicknamed the 'Black Rose' for some spice. Probably cloves."

Mike thought a minute. "There are whole bunches of Greeks around Europe. There were even some in Grantville, but I think most of them moved to Burgundy to work for Grand Duke Bernhard."

"That is not relevant!"

Tom sighed. "In these plays, believe me, she's Arabian." He picked up his clipboard. "Lo and behold! I just turned her brother into an *Arabian* merchant. Barely one stroke of the pen."

"She's not a queen, either."

Tom glared. "*The Arabian Sister of a Prosperous Merchant* doth not a workable title make."

* * *

"'I don't have time,' Massinger said."

The only times he came out of his room, these days, was for rehearsals and performances, when he had to be on stage. And for dinners with the two lords and a lady, which were command performances in their own right.

Christina got a manservant assigned to him full-time, to make sure that he ate other meals, slept, bathed, and occasionally changed his clothes.

He didn't have time to write the plays for the spring fair.

Or even look at the outlines.

Massinger was submerged in the misfortunes of Mary Hamilton at the court of Mary, Queen of Scots, in France, trying to write her tragedy before he lost track of it, while Elizabeth Tudor stomped through his brain, demanding her allotted share of his attention.

Or more. In another universe, the gentle Edward VI's doting older sister, renowned patron of arts and education, protector of scientists and scholars, the leader who brought England into a position at the pinnacle of world civilization, genius of the ecumenical movement, would become his greatest defender, spymistress, and admiral of the ocean seas all in one. Not every heroine could combine the most remarkable attributes of Gretchen Richter, Francisco Nasi, and John Chandler Simpson all in one, but Elizabeth of England insisted.

Nor would she remain a virgin—hypothetical or actual.

Massinger could see it now, as she led the great combined English and Spanish armada—yes, Don Juan of Austria would bring the Spanish contribution—into the eastern Mediterranean to confront the oncoming Turks. Mary in Naples had come through with badly needed reinforcements when it looked as if England's mightiest effort on behalf of a united Christendom might not suffice; Mary of Scotland had rallied the French Huguenots under Henry of Navarre to the Great Cause, shortly before the St. Bartholomew's Night massacre that never occurred.

So Tom filled in the outlines of the "Walter Plays," as everyone else in the troupe was calling them when they wanted to get anything accomplished. They were to the point that every time anyone mentioned *The Not-Arabian Not-a-Queen*, everyone broke out in giggles.

* * *

"If the USE had advance-censorship the way England does, I wouldn't be writing a play about Georg of Hesse-Darmstadt right now. Much less Friedrich of Hesse-Homburg."

"That is so true," was Dick's response. "But Lord Philipp's brother really was off in Berlin conspiring with Oxenstierna, so he was just as guilty as Georg."

"Which could get awkward if it's pointed out," Christina warned. Unless you're going for some kind of *Sippenhaft*, which I don't think is a good idea. Think of how much Eila was afraid of something like that—having relatives held accountable just for being related to an offender, even if they hadn't done anything themselves. In my opinion, it's definitely not a good idea to make Friedrich the secondary villain. Maybe you should just blend him into the rest of the dispossessed *Hochadel* from the Province of the Main—make that the nobles of never-never-land who supported the wrong side in Walter's rebellion."

But Friedrich of Hesse-Homburg *was* just as guilty as Georg, Tom thought.

What's more, he looked like a pig. He really did. There was a portrait of him in the gallery at Philippseck. The bushy hair with its center part, the round face, the huge popping eyes with beetling eyebrows, the pug nose. The black mustache with its upturned points; the double chin-ny-chin-chin with its tiny goatee. So unique.

So *individual*. The mustache was almost Snidely Whiplash quality. The points didn't extend quite as far, but Friedrich's face was fat. It would be so easy to duplicate Friedrich's face. It wouldn't even take a lot of stage make-up. And only a little extension of the mustache points.

Tom adored Rocky and Bullwinkle.

Ludovic could do the part justice. For all of his problems, Ludovic was an excellent actor.

Tom had a stubborn streak. Who was Christina to tell him what to write? They were on such a tight schedule that if he wrote it, she wouldn't have time to make him go back and change it.

He didn't get *The Arabian Queen, Part 2*, ready for rehearsal until they were in the attics of the big *Schloss* down in Butzbach, a week before the fair. Two weeks before the public performance.

So much for the hope he had expressed to Mrs. Mundell, back before Massinger's Men left Grantville, that the schedule would get less hectic.

Butzbach, Province of the Main
May 1637

Lorrie's boys, all four of them, could wield a hammer. Construct a stage set.

This led to the presumption that they could contribute to the construction of other things.

Heaven forbid that honored guests of high rank should stand in the streets of Butzbach to watch a play, down on the cobblestones with the *hoi polloi*.

Mike, Wolfgang, Zach, and Jim were far from the only guys drafted into the project. There were carpenters and cabinetmakers, journeymen and apprentices, a few day laborers (the town was small enough that it didn't have more than a few), and many other residents of Butzbach who had better things to do but couldn't refuse when Lord Philipp issued a declaration that something was going to happen.

Scaffolds. Plain raw lumber. A scaffold was a scaffold, after all. The four of them knocked in nails; they didn't have a problem keeping up with the professionals.

Mike took a look at what was going up next. "I thought it would be more like...you know...temporary outdoor seating."

These didn't even vaguely resemble the stands a guy saw on television, up on the sides of the streets of DC for the important people at a presidential inauguration or something: basically pre-fab metal piping joined together and planks to sit on.

They didn't even look like the pull-out bleachers in the gym at the Grantville high school.

More like...

"What do they look like? They remind me of something."

Somebody was still hammering, down underneath.

Zach considered. "Those fancy seats around the edge of a theater that I saw in the picture books in drama class? The ones fastened to the walls."

He was right. By the time those seats were done, the boards were gilded. Festooned. Draped with colored cloth. Banners flew from poles stuck into the support posts. Painted plaster cherubs, painted plaster unicorn heads, painted plaster griffins, painted plaster you-name-its—Lord Philipp must have had a warehouse full of the things.

Outdoor opera boxes. Enough of them for a couple of hundred people. Not separate, individual, boxes, though; they were all open to one another. With chairs. Not fixed benches. Chairs. Pretty crude chairs, but painted bright colors.

Mike wondered if Lord Philipp had gotten the idea from some medieval historical epic movie that he'd seen while he was in Grantville.

Then realized that the directors of medieval historical epic movies had probably gotten the idea from Lord Philipp and his ilk.

The steps came up from the back side, one at each end and one in the middle. The honored guests, all dressed up, would sort of parade in and take their places, which would probably be as entertaining for the rest of the crowd as the plays. No one could say that people didn't get their money's worth at the Butzbach spring fair.

Down underneath, a carpenter was reaming out an apprentice for doing something wrong.

The foreman of the job came around the corner. "What are you two shiftless laggards doing standing there? Move, you drowsy idlers! Are you lazy? Are you indolent? Are your minds dull? Are you incapable? Dallying to the point of taking Sloth as your mistress?"

They got back to work.

* * *

"*Schloss* Philippseck, Münster (not the one in Westphalia), bei Butzbach

"Tuesday

"Dear Mom,

"Like I said last week, we've really been driving ourselves into exhaustion to get three brand new plays ready in time for the spring fair, on top of all the extra work on the stands and such, but I think we've made it.

"We're doing the plays in the town of Butzbach, not out at Philippseck, because when people come to a fair—this one lasts a whole two weeks and attracts a lot of visitors—they want a chance to shop and eat food that they haven't cooked themselves, and the people who live in the town want a chance to sell them things. None of them really want to walk an extra couple of miles just to see a play.

"All of us are crammed into the attic of the *Landgrafenschloss* in town right now, because Lord Philipp has dozens (that's literal) of high-ranking guests just as crammed into Philippseck. 'Crammed' is literal, too. There are three couples sleeping on cots in our breakfast room. Along with their servants, who are sleeping wall-to-wall on straw pallets on the floor. We had to move all our stuff down into the wine cellars.

"We'll do the performances outside on the main street if the weather is decent; inside the St. Markus Church if not. There's not a market square, really, just the street with the *Wendelinkapelle* at the end of it and the *Spital* buildings. A person doesn't see churches made of *Fachwerk* all that often; most of them are stone. It will make a nice backdrop for the Walter plays, which are sort of medieval (if you make up your own version of medieval) and cut down a lot on the amount of sets and scrims that we'll have to get the staff here at the castle to haul a couple of miles.

"Sorry this is so short.

"Love you always, Mom,

"Jim"

* * *

Lord Philipp said to the margrave and margravine that he really hoped this worked.

The margrave and margravine replied with solemnity that they hoped so too, without specifying that their hopes were somewhat different.

They hoped very much that Philipp's tendency to put the best construction on everything wasn't going to get him in major trouble with Gustav Adolf, who was not in a forgiving mood when it came to anything connected to the Oxenstierna Plot.

So they had done what they could to see that things turned out a little differently than Philipp, perhaps, planned.

It would be so unfortunate if their long-time friend, host, and major source of financial support were perceived to be a supporter of the emperor's opponents.

That was the sort of thing that led to such unfortunate events as losing one's lands and money.

* * *

"*Schloss* Philippseck, Münster (not the one in Westphalia), bei Butzbach

"Friday

"Dear Mom,

"I'm sorry I didn't get this mailed on the regular schedule, but things got busy again.

"So far, we've only put on *The Mongol General*. That was this afternoon, and we lucked out on the weather: warm and sunny. I thought it went over real well. Since we were outside, we even had a couple of real horses for the Mongol horde (with a couple of Lord Philipp's grooms to hold their reins and be the Mongol horde). I was backstage, being thankful that there wasn't much wind, so all those banners up on poles didn't spook them.

Never trust a horse is one important lesson that I've learned since being down-time.

"Valentin Wagner, the artist staying at the *Landgrafenschloss* here in town, painted the rest of the Mongol horde on the front wall of one of the houses. The owner sort of liked the idea and said that we could use his house as part of the set for free if Wagner used paint that wouldn't wash off and he got to keep the mural.

"The play has colorful costumes, and it has archery. Yes, Mom, we put up a safe backdrop; Ludovic played Tristan and he wasn't aiming anywhere near the audience. It turns out that he's a pretty good shot with a longbow. I know we all have problems with him, but he's a real professional once he gets on stage.

"So after all the panic, I've taken a couple of deep breaths and may even dare to relax. I'm just glad that I'm backstage (except when they need an extra extra) rather than onstage.

"Get back to you later. I'm so tired that I've got to crash.

"Love you always,

"Jim"

* * *

In between the Friday of *The Mongol General* and the Tuesday of *The Arabian Queen, Part 1*, they managed a full, preliminary, start-to-finish, "dress rehearsal" for *Part 2*. "No reasonable person would call this a dress rehearsal," Mike protested. They were in the attic of the *Landgrafenschloss*.

"Do you think it's practical for Massinger's Men to rehearse on site? In the street? In the middle of the fair?" Christina slammed her hand against one of the support beams.

Philippine and Margarethe Lehr, on stage for several of the scenes and backstage during the rest of them, got a pretty good...that might be, devastatingly clear...idea of just what the play would be revealing.

The instant Dick dismissed the cast, they went down the stairs with reasonable decorum and then, the minute they were well out of sight of the Schloss, started to run.

Their father had to know about this.

Arndt Lehr pulled off his schoolteacher hat, grabbed his CoC organizer hat, and went— walking rapidly, to be sure, but not running—to talk to the captain of the Butzbach city militia.

The Butzbach CoC and the Butzbach city militia being, essentially, one and the same as far as membership was concerned.

Lehr and Johann Ronstadt spent the evening pondering these things over their beers. The rate of pondering was accelerated by their having known one another since they were born. Or, at least, since Lehr was born, Ronstadt having preceded him into the world by a couple of years. It was pretty hard not to know other people well in a town the size of Butzbach.

"It bothered me a lot, about those kids," Ronstadt said. "The ones His Lordship took in and Eila ran away with, because she was afraid." His day job was keeper of the *Spital*. "The columns that came in from the east wouldn't have been killing persecutors if there hadn't been persecutions to start with."

Lehr chewed on his mustache.

Ronstadt pondered on. "Some of these people that young Quiney is fingering in the play because they were off in Berlin..."

Lehr emitted a helpful drone of *ummmm*.

"Like the counts at Idstein and Büdingen..."

"*Ja*, both of them."

"They're on the guest list that Lord Philipp sent down from the castle."

"Are they, now?"

"It wouldn't cause me a bit of pain to see them caught. Arrested and put on trial."

"Sort of what I was thinking."

"What good is a city gate if you can't close it?"

"None, if you're trying to keep someone out."

"It works the other way around, too. If you need to keep someone in."

"Do you think we need to mention it to the mayor?"

"Lienert Lotz is a worrier. Most likely, it would just worry him."

"*Ja*. It would."

"Now Gertraud, though..." Gertraud Kreckerin was the mayor's wife.

"Might not hurt to drop a word. There'll be ladies present, after all. And children."

"Do you think that Isaac Lederer might have any ideas?"

Ronstadt pondered a bit longer.

Lehr switched to chewing on the other side of his mustache.

"I see him every now and then," Ronstadt finally admitted. "Especially around fair time. Things can always get a bit touchy when there are outsiders in town. People who don't understand how we manage things here."

"Ummmm."

"Nobody would think it was odd if I dropped by his shop."

The Butzbach city militia, charged with maintaining order during the spring fair, received a few additional instructions in regard to procedures.

Gertraud mentioned to her friends Leis Orthin, Katharina Rehin, and Gela Rießin, each of whom happened to be married to a city councilman, that having those horses so close to the crowd during the Mongol play last week had made her nervous about a child getting under the feet of one of them, so in case the players pulled a stunt like that again, there ought to be some kind of a plan for moving visitors away from right in front of the stage, so they didn't get pushed back against the viewing stands for Lord Philipp's important guests. Somebody might get hurt.

Lederer gladly put the Butzbach Jewish Defense League, such as it was, all twenty or so, at Ronstadt's disposal.

"I'll think of someplace," Ronstadt said, "where nobody will be expecting you to be. Those are always the best places to have somebody be, so to speak."

* * *

"*Schloss* Philippseck, Münster (not the one in Westphalia), bei Butzbach

"Tuesday (again; it's a different Tuesday from the last one, I'm pretty sure. The days are all running into each other.)

"Dear Mom,

"One more play done this afternoon. The *Arabian Queen, Part 1.* Lots of fancy costumes, again. Christina is really hoping that when we finish this visit, Lord Philipp will decide that he doesn't need a lot of costumes hanging around his castle and will let us take them with us, wherever we end up going next. I'm not sure that Master Massinger even knows, because we can hardly get him to surface from writing except to act when we absolutely need him.

"We did need him to be the Mongol general, and he did a fabulous job. For *Part 1,* today, he only had to be Walter's grandfather, and it wasn't a big part. Tom let the old man live long enough to see his grandson's triumphant return from his adventures. In *Part 2,* Massinger only shows up in the very last scene, to be the king and give the hero a medal. I don't think that he's even bothered to read any of the scripts except for the scenes where he has lines.

"I hope the Tudors are worth all the time and effort he's giving them. At least the first one starts after Edward VI has already succeeded to the throne, so when we stage them, we won't have to deal with Henry the Fattest and the Six Wives.

"If we did, maybe the margrave could play Henry.

"That was a joke.

"Master Massinger says that he—the margrave that is—didn't used to be so heavy, but that the last few years, since Tilly's army threw him out of Magdeburg, he hasn't had much else to do except eat. He does keep moving, though, and just having us around is giving him a few more things to do.

"I'll get this in the mail, now.

"Love you always, Mom.

"Jim"

* * *

It was an impressive procession, Lord Philipp and his guests coming through the gates and into town for the play. With trumpeters, even. And men in fancy livery who were actually bodyguards. The margrave and Lady Dorothea on his right hand, for even the most impecunious of margraves outranked a landgrave. On his left, Landgrave George of Hesse-Darmstadt with his wife and three young children and their nannies (three more, deemed too young for the play, had been left up at Philippseck with other nannies). With attendants. Someone had even managed to dig up a few ladies-in-waiting for the occasion.

To the right of the margrave, Landgrave Friedrich of Hesse-Homburg with wife and five young children, ladies, nannies, and guards. To the left of George of Hesse Darmstadt, Governor Brahe of the Province of the Main (whose wife was in Finland, everybody knew), and, to make the numbers match, Anselm Keller, the head of the Fourth of July Party in the province (who wasn't even married). The group accompanying them, Brahe's advisers (mostly military) and Keller's colleagues (mostly political), notably lacked children and nannies. And ladies, for that matter. Brahe's attendants numbered none; Keller's only two.

"Why not the head of the Crown Loyalists?" a girl in the crowd asked her mother. For which she got an exasperated look and an impatient, "The governor *is* the head of the Crown Loyalists in the province. They're displaying unity, or something. I think that's what the newspaper said."

That group was directed to the center steps leading up to the seats.

Behind them, there came a group of miscellaneous counts—those generally lumped together geographically as "counts of the Wetterau," even though the Wetterau was not and never had been a county with a count. Three Nassau brothers with various suffixes, Wiesbaden, Idstein, Weilburg. Wolfgang Heinrich von Isenburg-Büdingen. Several more, all of whom had been early Protestant allies of the king of Sweden when he intervened in the war, and none of whom had approved of the direction things had taken since the up-timers arrived. Most with wives and several children (aged anywhere from mid-twenties down to about six; any younger than that were either up at Philippseck with nannies or had been left at home, also with nannies). Attendants, ladies-in-waiting, and guards. They were politely ushered toward the end steps on Lord Philipp's right.

Followed by miscellaneous dignitaries, provincial officials, military officers, mayors of neighboring towns, and random hangers-on who had managed to wangle an invitation into the stands somehow, many with families. Those went to the steps on the left.

Act I went smoothly. Most of Lord Philipp's guests had been present for the play the week before, so they were expecting Denmark, and Denmark, technically, was what they got. Even if it did bear a closer resemblance to some strange hybrid of England and never-never-land. Walter of Gurnie, although grieving that his wife was not with him, started out on the heroics that would be needed to put an end to some problems facing the king.

The day was warm and sunny. In the stands and on the streets, the honored guests and ordinary fair-goers consumed enough beer to make the brewers of Butzbach happy men and women.

Nobody in Massinger's Men, no matter how exasperating they found him, denied that Ludovic could put on a good show when it came to physical action. He leaped, he bounded, he strutted, he waved a prop sword around with flourishes. There was a conspiracy against the king, but he was still in the process of trying to identify the villains.

Act II went even better. Most of the time, Maryam and Mahmoud were traveling, seeking to follow Walter. Lots of pretty girls, lots of quasi-oriental costumes, even a couple of songs. All of it appealed to the fair-goers.

Act III opened with a scene in which the villainous conspirators had gathered and were villainously conspiring against the king and the lovely regent who held one of the nation's provinces in his name.

Snidely Whiplash might have provided inspiration to Tom for more than just a mustache.

It began to dawn on various people in the stands just what was being revealed. The names might have been changed, but the events were appallingly familiar and marched right along, one after the other. Not to mention that the actor portraying the second of the main conspirators wore make-up and mustaches that caused him to resemble, really to an extraordinary extent...

This particular Georg and that specific Friedrich moved to leave—actually jumped up, gathered their guards, and made a brisk trot in the direction of the steps, seriously impeded by the gaggle of ladies-in-waiting and nannies who had been seated to their rear.

They weren't the only people who noticed the meaning of the on-stage dialogue and actions.

Brahe and Keller moved to intercept them. As did a number of the military officers and civilian factotums who had come with them.

The counts of the Wetterau turned to scramble down the right-hand steps, only to be blocked, their progress impeded by the billowing skirts of even more ladies-in-waiting and a positive plethora of nannies, none of whom could get down the steps to move out of the way of the oncoming counts. The steps were, in turn, blocked by the Butzbach city militia. Ronstadt's additional instructions had been, basically, "Nobody's getting out of those stands, men."

Which was a good idea in principle, but, by and large, once the fleeing counts had gotten through it couldn't be put into practice. (Their body-guards threw quite a large pile of nannies and ladies-in-waiting over the guard rail, where they and their petticoats seriously interfered with the militia's movements—a move that Ronstadt had not anticipated at all.)

The counts abandoned their families in the stands, and, surrounded by their bodyguards, made a fighting retreat toward the gates.

Which were closed and locked—at Ronstadt's orders "the instant you hear any kind of noise coming from down by the *Wendelinkapelle*"—with an eye to keeping any guilty anybody from getting out of town.

Since he had limited manpower at his disposal, he had armed the Jewish Defense League from the city Zeughaus and assigned them to that task. There weren't a lot of them, but he figured that there were enough to pull the gates closed, fasten them, and get into the guardhouses.

He got more than he bargained for. By and large, for the couple of centuries of its existence, the Jewish community in Butzbach had lived by trading in cattle and leather goods. They also had a small kosher slaugh-terhouse and a butcher shop. They had chains; they had pulleys; they had wrought-iron hooks in multiple sizes. The spaces before the gates blossomed with some interesting obstacles.

Isaac Lederer's oldest nephew, who had been to Grantville, looked around at their improvisations and said, "I have absolutely no idea how they managed these things in those up-time westerns. Towns with no walls at all: how ridiculous."

Blocked from the gate exits, the various counts of the Wetterau and their bodyguards made a retreat toward the city walls, intending to fort up in the tower that someday in the future, for reasons that remained a mystery to the residents of Butzbach in the present time, would be described as the *Hexenturm*.

Lederer had no instructions in this regard. Leaving only a couple men at each gate, he took the other dozen or so available to him and made a stand at the tower's entrance. Lacking weapons expertise, but well supplied with heavy chains with hooks on the end, they managed to keep the counts out until the militia had time to come up behind and box them in.

In front of the viewing stands, instead of guests watching Act III, the players had stopped trying to perform and instead were watching what was going on with the guests.

Or prudently trying to back into the houses behind them to hide, depending on their individual temperaments.

"At least, there aren't many kids in the cast of this one," Anna Maria said to Philippine. "Just a few as extras in the adoring crowd. And the king hadn't shown up to award the medals yet, so we know that Master Massinger is safe."

The fair-going crowd was scattering, with, really, no place to go, since the gates were closed. The city council-wives moved in to funnel them down certain streets and in specific directions, where there was a little space.

"At least," Tom said, "there's no shooting."

"So far."

Horst was under the stands, sorting out various injuries to overtipped nannies and ladies-in-waiting. It wasn't as bad as he had expected: all those petticoats had provided some cushioning when they landed and the fall wasn't more than eight feet, even accounting for being tossed up-and-over a bit to clear the guard rail.

Up in the stands, Georg and Friedrich hadn't even made it as far as the steps. There were flailing fists, ducking wives and ladies-in-waiting, screaming children, battling bodyguards, and what appeared to observers to be total chaos. Close encounters of a messy kind.

It kind of broke up when the portly Margrave Christian Wilhelm climbed up on one of the chairs and, with a war cry and ferocious leap, launched himself down upon the equally hefty Landgrave Friedrich—and promptly died of a heart attack. His sheer weight kept Friedrich pinned, and once he was down, his guards focused on protecting his family from injury.

From the stage across the street, Ludovic erupted in an enthusiastic shout of, "Great move; good going!" Those who had not fled—most of them males between the ages of thirteen and thirty who enjoyed a good prize fight or bear baiting, even a barroom brawl every now and then—took up the chant.

By the time the piles of bodies were sorted out, the landgrave of Hesse-Darmstadt and landgrave of Hesse-Homburg had been taken into custody by the governor of the Province of the Main, the member of parliament assisting.

The military officers went off to see what on earth was going on over by the city walls and put a stop to it. The civilian officials went off to look for the mayor and find out what on earth he thought his militia was doing.

Ronstadt and Lehr broke the news to all of them that the militia of Butzbach was also the CoC in Butzbach and had, in cooperation with the

JDL, taken into custody several noble practitioners of high treason against the emperor, whom they would turn over only to the governor and only upon receiving assurances that they would be brought to justice publicly, promptly, and with no deference to their rank.

Landgrave Philipp patted the margravine on the back, uttered some soothing words, and started to try to figure out how to get all the wives, children, ladies, nannies, and other tattered and occasionally bloody remaining company of his honored guests back where they belonged.

That evening, as he sat despondently in his study, Lord Philipp mourned the outcome. Margravine Dorothea walked up behind him, gave his shoulders a comforting hug, and said, "I'm sure that no one will blame you."

She sincerely hoped that General Brahe would conclude that the whole fair, and specifically the final performance, had been a clever ploy orchestrated by Philipp to draw in a group of "too big to fail" plotters and make them reveal themselves to the forces of imperial justice.

With luck, Philipp and Christian Wilhelm would get medals out of it themselves.

Christian Wilhelm's would be posthumous, unfortunately. Which meant that she would now have a year of official, formal, mourning to get through.

Of course, she could go back to Magdeburg. Maybe she should. With Elisabeth Sofie's marriage this spring, her daughter would be needing a chaperone. Since they had been Philipp's guests, she had managed to save most of the subsidy that was coming in from Duke Johann of Saxe-Altenburg.

As soon as things calmed down a bit, here, she would suggest to Philipp that perhaps she would benefit from a change of scene. Surely, if she went to Magdeburg, there would be an opportunity for her to suggest to Mrs. Simpson that it would be a nice idea to hint to Gustav that Christian

Wilhelm and Philipp should be recognized for their services in revealing treason. Possibly with a pension for the grieving widow.

* * *

"*Schloss* Philippseck, Münster (not the one in Westphalia), bei Butzbach

"Friday

"Dear Mom,

"Things are absolutely crazy right now.

"It looks like we'll be coming back to Grantville. Like, next week.

"Do you remember, I said that I didn't think that Master Massinger had read any of the scenes except for his own lines? I was right.

"Apparently, it was a little bit too obvious (to anyone who knew the background) just who the villains were in *The Arabian Queen, Part 2* the way Tom wrote it. Like, the guy who attempted to usurp the throne was Oxenstierna and the main villain conspiring with him was Land-grave Georg of Hesse-Darmstadt, who is Lord Philipp's *nephew*. And that this particular Georg (as distinguished from all the other Georgs in the country) and one particular Friedrich (as distinguished from all the other Friedrichs in the country), who happens to be Lord Philipp's *brother*, even before Oxenstierna, came pretty close to pulling off a 'none dare call it treason' coup against the lady who is the regent in the Province of Hesse and a good friend of the emperor. Also, that the rest of the conspirators were a bunch of counts who are Lord Philipp's *neighbors*.

"So, up there on the stage, in the bright sunshine, in front of a big crowd, with special guests watching, the actors said all this. Out in the super-fancy stands that Lord Philipp had us build, the special guests included 'that' Georg and 'that' Friedrich. They also included General Nils Brahe, who is Gustav Adolf's governor of the Province of the Main, who came with Anselm Keller, who's the head of the Fourth of July Party in the province.

"Apparently they had something to say, right then and there.

"The margrave had another heart attack, and died right in the middle of it all. At least that put an end to the big fight. I'm mentioning the fight because I suppose it's too much to hope that you won't read about it in the newspaper. None of us (Wolf, Zach, Mike, or me) was involved. I promise. The fight was up in the stands; we were either backstage or in the wings, waiting to be extras in the adoring crowd that was preparing to applaud Walter the Triumphant Hero when he showed up.

"The margravine is making sure that it's Lord Philipp who gets credit for the Big Reveal, and there are lots of compliments about how noble and patriotic he was to do it, sort of the way people talked about the mother and brother of that Unabomber guy when they turned him in a few years ago—well, a few years before the Ring of Fire happened, but you know what I mean. It was mostly the margrave who talked to Tom, but she's not pushing that at all.

"Christina and Dick and Tom covered for the margrave and Master Massinger real well, I thought, when Lord Philipp came storming down.

"But Lord Philipp 'suggested' that Massinger's Men might want to go back to Grantville. Like Real Soon Now! That's going to cut off two of the months he agreed to pay Master Massinger when we came. At least, he wants to get rid of us bad enough that he's paying for the freight wagons.

"We should get home about the middle of June, if we get everything packed up tomorrow, which is what he wants us to do, and he says Christina can borrow as many of the palace staff as she needs to. The captain of the guards—he's a great guy—says that he'll open up the outdoor entrance to the cellars. We have it all stored down there because we used it as a rehearsal space. So we can just bring the wagons in, load them there, and bring them out when we're done. There's plenty of headroom for those Conestoga-wagon type covers that the freighters use to keep the loads dry.

"I'll put this in the mail tonight, anyway, because the postal couriers move a lot faster than we will.

"Do you have any idea if there's someplace pretty cheap where we'll be able to stash four wagon loads of sets and props and costumes and stuff until Master Massinger gets reorganized? They're pretty big wagons.

"Love you always, Mom,

"Jim"

More McDonalds

Terry Howard

This story follows "Bremen or Bust" in Issue 9 and "Clan McDonald" in Issue 11.

Officer Lyndon Johnson walked through the green front door of Club 250 in the middle of the lunch rush. The bar was not half as full as it used to be. More and more people were leaving town, joining the military, or drinking elsewhere with coworkers who weren't welcome in the club, especially younger men or boys who were coming of age. It was late May 1635. Lyndon was still wearing his military-style greatcoat, but it was not buttoned up, and his head and hands were bare.

"Lyndon," Ken called out cheerfully from behind the bar, seeing one of his favorite young men come in. "What's up?"

"We need Jimmy Dick down at the hospital," the young police officer answered the older bartender and owner of the bar.

Jimmy looked up and into the mahogany-framed mirror behind the bar. He turned to Lyndon, his face full of concern. "What's wrong? Who's hurt? Was there a problem at the mine?" Two of his roommates worked the coal.

"No. Everything is fine. Well, here at least," Lyndon replied. "But they've got that kid Hans picked up on the road into town the other day while he was coming back from checking out a complaint. And I mean literally on the road. Hans first radioed that he had a dead man in the road. Then he said the man was still breathing and he was taking him to the hospital. Let's go," Lyndon said to Jimmy.

"Why me?" Jimmy asked.

"Because," Lyndon replied, "he's one of yours."

"Shit!" Jimmy said. He upended his beer bottle to the antique metal-tray ceiling and chugged until it was empty before sliding off the bar stool and heading for his coat hanging on a wall peg.

"What makes him mine?" Jimmy asked.

Lyndon sighed as he held the door for the semi-reformed reprobate. "When Hans got him to the hospital, he was out of it. Hans says he didn't weigh more than a hundred pounds, that he looked about twelve years old, and that he was barefoot and dressed in rags that barely covered his body. And other than a wheellock pistol and a big knife, he didn't have a thing with him. He was suffering from exposure, starvation, dehydration, and a high fever. And if they'd been busy enough to triage, they would have let him die. But things were slow, so they got a feeding tube down him and gave him something for the fever, got him cleaned up and into a warm bed. That was three days ago. He's finally started coming to. He hasn't said much, but he says he's a McDonald, and he wanted to know if he was in time for the invasion."

"Shit," Jimmy said, getting into the panda. The Grantville police still had black and white cruisers left from before the Ring of Fire. "We sent out letters to everywhere we could think of telling everyone not to come."

"Well, it seems this kid didn't read his mail," Lyndon said, turning the key in the ignition. "How's things working out with the new baby in the house?" he asked, changing the topic.

"Jamey Ann is a little princess." Jimmy's toothy smile lit up his face like a proud grandpa. "She hardly ever cries. And she's tracking sounds and movement with her eyes. If I didn't know better, I'd think that she recognizes me. But the truth is she smiles and gurgles to anyone who picks her up and talks sweet to her. Old Lady McDee didn't want to let go of her and only gave her up when she got wet and had to be changed. We've had Asa and Dory over to dinner every Sunday since Ann and Jamey got home from the hospital. When Dory got to hold Jamey, she finally stopped talking about going to Bremen next month. Now the way she carries on, you'd think she was the baby's grandmother."

Lyndon smirked but kept his mouth shut, mostly anyway, "Yeah, well, there's a lot of that going around."

Jimmy got a twinkle in his eye and laughed. "Yes. I guess there is at that."

Lyndon took a route to the hospital that avoided the downtown part of Grantville. The public safety vehicles were exempt from the dawn-to-dusk ban on vehicular traffic downtown, but that was no reason to drive down a pedestrian-dominated main street when there wasn't any need.

The hospital parking lot, paved to hold a whole congregation's worth of cars back when the hospital was still a church, was mostly empty. Even with gas for sale at the gas stations, a lot of cars were still sitting idle. Tires were an issue—a lot of them went bad while sitting that long. Batteries were expensive and so was fuel. The trolley system was cheap and easy to use, so why fuss with a car? The expanded building now took up most of the unpaved land that the church once owned. Lyndon got out and went in with Jimmy. He had been instructed by his boss, Chief Richards, to see to it that Jimmy took responsibility for the young Scotsman.

The floor nurse, a white-haired matron, a stiffly starched cap perched on her head, spotted them and met them in the hall. "Thank goodness you're here," she said in relief. "I hope you can calm the lad down and convince him to stay put. He's worried about running up a bill he can't pay. We *told* him the local McDonalds would cover his hospital bill, but he's still worried about it."

Jimmy mumbled, "Shit, people sure are free with spending my hard-earned money."

Lyndon laughed softly. "Hard-earned money? When was the last time you did a day's work, Jimmy? Not since right after the flash of light when you chipped in to help get the new railroad track laid from the mine to the power plant. Now all you do is collect the rent off of half the buildings downtown, and Lamb Properties does the actual collecting for you."

"Well, it's still my money everyone else is spending."

The nurse paid the two of them no heed at all but talked over and through the conversation as if it never happened. "And he's afraid the McDonald army will leave town without him, so he's insisting we release him. He isn't ready to leave, and we'll tie him down if we have to."

"How is he doing?" Lyndon asked.

"He's alive," she answered, with a residue of surprise in her voice. "And that is saying something. You can count every rib he has, clear as day. He hasn't been eating well for the last year if ever. I don't see how he didn't have frostbite on his feet, being bare in this weather, but his callouses are so thick he might as well have been wearing shoes, I guess. I don't think his feet know what shoes are. He's weak as a kitten and as stubborn as a mule. He doesn't want to answer questions. We barely have a name; we don't know where he's from other than he speaks English with what I'm told is a London dockside gutter accent. He wants out of here, and he wants to join the McDonald army. We had to fetch his pistol and that sword he had before he'd calm down and quit worrying that they were stolen. Once he saw them, he was okay with us putting them back in lockup, with the promise he could have them when he left."

"But you did get a name out of him?"

"Yes, he said he was Charles McDonald," the nurse replied.

"Great. Another Charles." Jimmy said with an air of disgust. "It seems like every other McDonald is named Charles. Now I've got three of them. I take it it's the equivalent of Hans for the Krauts."

"If you two will come this way, I'll take you to him." They followed the woman in her bright white uniform down the hall of white-painted walls and shiny waxed oaken floors. "We've got him in a private room because we didn't expect him to make it. Having a roommate die can upset a whole ward full of patients."

In the room, a petite blonde high school volunteer was sitting in the wooden armchair keeping an eye on the sullen young man, making sure he stayed in bed. Apparently wearing nothing but a hospital gown tied in the back wasn't enough to keep the boy under the sheet and woolen blanket. He'd kicked the sheet and blanket off as if they were too hot to put up with. It was Saturday, so the volunteer wasn't skipping school. She was dressed in the same starched white uniform as the nurse, except she didn't have a hat and there was blue trim on the skirt. She'd given up trying to engage him in conversation and was reading a book aloud. "—but viewing that the wench strove to depart, and Don Quixote labored to withhold her, the jesting seemed—"

"Thank you, Elizabeth." The floor nurse said to the volunteer. "These gentlemen need to talk with our patient." She turned to the boy in the bed. "Charles, this is Officer Lyndon Johnson." She waved at the policeman. "And this is the man you came looking for." She pointed at Jimmy Dick. "Lord James Shaver, the war leader for the local Clan McDonald. Please do not make us roust out The McDonald himself. The old man is in frail health and refuses to quit working. He needs his evening to relax. But if you can't work out your problems with Lord James, we *will* bring in Laird Asa to set you straight." She glanced at Lyndon. "We will leave you gentlemen to your business. Come, Elizabeth."

Jimmy looked the boy over. He wasn't as bad as a picture of a holocaust victim, but he would do until one turned up. His reddish hair was cropped close to help deal with lice, since they couldn't run him through the decontamination station downstairs and had to settle for a bed bath. There was a faint trace of freckles promising a full crop come summer. Jimmy guessed the lad to be maybe five feet, and if he weighed a pound over ninety, it sure didn't show. He looked to be all of twelve years old. "Charles," Jimmy said to the boy who was busy looking back at him in apprehension, "for my sins, it seems that I am now *Lord* James Richard Shaver, the war leader for the local Clan McDonald, such as it is. How old are you, boy?"

"Sixteen, sir."

Jimmy silently stared at the lad and waited.

"Well, fifteen." The boy conceded.

Jimmy continued to stare.

The lad grimaced and finally added, "Almost, anyway."

At last, Jimmy nodded. "So, you claim to the fourteen, and you look like you might be eleven or twelve?"

"Lord, I might be small for my age. But I swear on my mother's grave that I am just shy of fifteen."

"So your mother is dead. Where are you from, boy?"

"I'm a McDonald, sir."

"I'll give you that much. No one would admit it if they didn't have to. But that does not answer my question. You are not from the northern isles.

I know that accent. And you aren't from the clan in Ireland. I know that accent too. So where are you from?"

"London, my lord."

"Whether or not I am *your* lord is yet to be settled, boy. So far you are a stray stick figure of a lad who claims to be a McDonald. But you aren't from any of the clans. If you were, they never would have let you get into the shape you're in or let you go traipsing off at the end of the winter to come to Grantville. What were you doing in London?"

"Surviving, your grace."

"I'll answer to Lord James, boy, and if you're lucky maybe someday I'll let you think of me as 'my lord.' But call me 'your grace' again, and I'm out of here, and you are on your own. Is that clear?"

"Yes, you—, m—, yes Lord James."

"Now what were you doing in London? And don't say surviving, because it's clear to me that you weren't."

"Momma worked as a weaver until the fever took her. I worked her loom for a bit until the owner came back after the fever was over, and he found a country lass to work the loom. After that, I scrounged the docks and waterside when the tide was out."

"And what changed?" Jimmy asked.

"I took up with a girl who worked for an old man who ran a gang, mostly pickpockets, mostly kids. He was going to sell the girl to a brothel, so she ran away. I helped her learn the ins and outs of picking the tidal mudflats, and she shared my nest. Then her gang caught up with her and beat her to death. They were looking for me for stealing her, so I needed to run. I heard that the McDonalds of Grantville were raising an army and any McDonald was welcome. I knew where I could pinch a pistol, and I stowed away on a boat bound for Hamburg. Then I headed this way."

"And your only claim to being a McDonald is your claim that your mother told you so?" Jimmy asked.

"Yes, Lord James. But you need fighting men, and I want the five acres you're promising to everyone who signs up."

"I see." James stared at the boy for a while, and the lad squirmed like a live bug pinned to a collection card. In the end, James sighed and nodded. "Okay. I will acknowledge that you can think of me as 'my lord.' But I never want to hear it. And I sure don't want to hear 'your grace.' That will be enough to get you disowned. I'll answer to Lord James but I'd rather you called me Jimmy Dick or Mr. Shaver if you can't handle Jimmy Dick. But Lord James or Lord Jimmy will do. Is that clear?"

"Yes, sir."

"Now, first of all, you will quit giving the hospital staff problems. You will be a perfect patient. Don't worry about the bill. It is covered, and yes, you will work it off or pay it back. Can you read and write?"

"No, Lord James."

"We will see to that."

"Why?" The boy looked genuinely puzzled. "What would I ever do with that? I'm no priest or gentry."

"Because I said so. Because this is Grantville and here you will go to school until you are at least sixteen. Because we have an odd definition of gentleman here. A gentleman means you have manners and act politely. It has nothing to do with noble birth, and since you just became part of my household, part of my family, I will insist that you learn to be a gentleman by local standards. And because when you have learned to read you will be surprised at the world that will suddenly open up to you."

"But a fighting man doesn't need to read and write. And a farmer with five acres doesn't need it either."

"Lad, there is no army. We are not planning on conquering a homeland for the clan. So you are going to have to learn a trade, and in Grantville, I am not going to be able to get you an apprenticeship if you can't read."

"Sir, if you don't need fighting men, then why are you taking me in?"

Jimmy looked at Lyndon. "I find myself asking the same question. But I have a feeling that this man and his boss would have a few choice words with me if I didn't. I think the bottom line is that you need help and I have been elected as the man best able to provide that help."

"You can afford it, Jimmy," Lyndon said.

Jimmy never took his eyes off of Lyndon. "From each according to his ability, to each according to his needs. Is that the case, Lyndon?"

"I don't think that is exactly how Chief Richards would put it, Jimmy."

"No. I don't suppose he would. But that pretty much sums it up, doesn't it?"

Lyndon stood mute and, if the truth be told, a little red in the face.

"As a personal philosophy, it isn't that bad of one," Jimmy said barely audibly. "It just doesn't work well for a large group or multiple generations. Someone needs to take care of those who can't take care of themselves. I guess that's part and parcel of what it means to be part of a clan. And whether I want it or not, I guess Grantville's greatest philosopher is now famous for being part of the Grantville sept of Clan McDonald."

Jimmy looked back to the boy in the bed. "I've already got two guys answering to 'Charles' at home; don't need a third one."

Lyndon looked concerned, and panic flashed across the boy's face.

"So, until further notice, you will answer to 'London.' Is that clear?"

The relieved lad nodded.

"Okay. For now, your job is to get stronger. And I suggest you get that pretty little girl to teach you the alphabet, so you've got a jump on learning to read." He looked at a likewise relieved police officer. "Lyndon, let's get out of here and let London get some rest."

When they left the room, the floor nurse was back at the counter and her workstation. Elizabeth headed back to the room to keep watch. When she sat down and started reading aloud London startled her. "Lass, Lord James tells me that I must learn to read. Can you teach me?"

She looked at the suddenly changed demeanor of the patient. "Well, we can get started on it, I guess. Let me get a clipboard and some paper. I'll be right back."

At the counter, Elizabeth said, "Nurse Marta—"

"Is he up again?" the nurse said with clear frustration. "You should have just called out."

"No, ma'am. He's in bed and calm as can be. But his lord told him he must learn to read, and he asked me to teach him, so I need a clipboard and paper to get started."

"Well, that is almost a miracle."

When the hospital released London, the boy settled in on the couch in the living room, where Anna could keep an eye on him while he finished recovering. Elizabeth stopped by after school each day to continue his education. Anna brought down the bilingual Doctor Seuss books Jimmy had bought for the nursery. Shortly, London had them memorized in English and German and read through them daily before tackling something harder. It wasn't long before Elizabeth became Eli. She was sixteen, but London seemed older than he was, so she didn't seem to mind the age difference.

* * *

While London was still in the hospital, Lyndon stepped through the door of Club 250 around four o'clock. Ken wasn't behind the bar. But Jimmy Dick, in his usual blue jeans, white shirt, and tan cardigan sweater, was enthroned on his usual bar stool, slowly working on his usual endless bottle of beer.

"Jimmy?" Lyndon called out.

"Is the kid okay, Lyndon?" Jimmy turned around and slipped off the bar stool.

"Yeah, last I knew."

Jimmy drained the last swallow out of the bottom of his bottle and set the empty on the bar behind him without looking. "What's up?"

"I'm here to give you a ride to the train station." Lyndon mostly succeeded in suppressing a smile.

"Let me guess. You've found another McDonald!?" Jimmy sneered.

"Something like that." Lyndon smiled.

"It ain't fair, Lyndon."

"If anyone told you life was fair, they were lying, Jimmy."

Jimmy growled but grabbed his coat. The two men were silent for the brief trip to the train station; Lyndon wore a smirk and Jimmy affected a scowl.

At the station, they heard the train long before they saw it. It wasn't the usual train noises. It was a calm day, but the train sounded like the worst howling windstorm one could imagine. When it came into clear view, the reason for the noise was clear. Two kilted pipers were standing on top of a rail carriage, bending the air with a squeeze of a bag, fingers dancing on a chanter while another three reeds drearily droned away. As the train drew closer, the people at the station could hear the beat of a bodhran underneath the screaming pipes. The drummer was standing in the steps of the car. The pipers on the roof stopped with a flourish as the train came to a halt. The drummer continued, and a much gentler rendition of the song came through the open windows of the railcar. The drummer stopped when the music of the small pipes ended.

"Could someone be telling me where we could be finding Lord James of Clan McDonald?" one of the pipers on the roof called out.

"Here he is," Lyndon said loudly, with a wave of his arm that ended up pointing at Jimmy.

"Lord James, could you be using two more pipers for the coming campaign?" the piper on the roof asked.

The drummer stepped down, followed by a man carrying the small pipes under his arm, and a claymore—the two-handed kind that stretched from chin to floor—over his shoulder. The drummer had a basket-hilted sword and a targe hanging over the hilt. Both were wearing kilts, and not the up-time skirt, but a great kilt that is just a large piece of fabric folded into pleats and wrapped around under a belt.

"Didn't you get the letter? There isn't going to be a campaign," Jimmy shouted.

"What letter?" came the reply from the roof.

"The letter we sent to any McDonald sept or clan holding we could think of that might be heading this way. There is no invasion planned. So, no one is getting five acres."

"Oh, that's the problem. No, we never got your letter because we're Clan Cameron."

"Shit! First I have to deal with every stray McDonald who comes along, and now I've got camera men playing bagpipes."

The pipers on the roof climbed down, and two more kilted fellows appeared from the car, schlepping baggage, including two more claymores.

Someone in the livery of the Holiday Lodge, wearing white pants and dark blue jacket with the logo on the breast, was chatting with the small piper and the drummer. The pair started up a song. It was soft—mellow and pleasant. The second piper, who was just reaching the ground, began to sing in a fine tenor voice in something other than English. The steward from the lodge who was there to meet the train glanced at the singer and then started nodding in time to the music. As he listened, he took a business card out of his pocket, wrote a note on the back, and handed it to the tenor with a few words of explanation.

Jimmy turned to Lyndon. "They ain't McDonalds. So, they aren't mine. Right?"

"I don't think the chief will see it that way, Jimmy. They're here to join up. He'll figure they're yours. You'll have to walk them over to the pharmacy for a quarantine check. Moss and Little agreed to take care of it for train passengers, since they are so close to the station."

"Quarantine check? When did that start?"

"Since London showed up with a fever. Anybody from England should be checked until further notice."

"Mr. Shaver?" The steward from the Holiday Lodge seemed to appear out of nowhere at Jimmy's elbow.

"What do you want?" Jimmy snarled.

"The musicians said I would need to talk to you. They will have to audition, of course, but that won't be a problem. I'm sure the director will want them when he's heard them."

"What?" Confusion overshadowed the snarl.

"The lodge needs a new dinner act, and they'll be perfect." He handed Jimmy one of the business cards that he seemed to have in endless numbers. "So if they're available, call this number and ask for the program director. And there's my client. I've got to go." Which he did.

Jimmy sighed. "Well, let's get you guys cleaned up to start with, and then we'll have to figure out what to do with you. At least some of you have a job waiting."

They insisted on making music while they walked, and of course that got them noticed.

Jimmy, have you got a kilt?

One week later, when Lyndon answered a summons to the chief's office, the chief was sitting behind his clutter-free desk perusing a letter. The chief looked up and very solemnly asked, "How would you feel about going to Bremen?"

"Not interested," Lyndon replied.

"Too bad. I was hoping you would see it as a vacation. It seems that Jimmy Dick is now identified as the war chief for the local Clan McDonald. If Laird Asa and Dory aren't going, someone in Magdeburg is of the opinion that it has to be Jimmy, or the people kicking up a fuss will think we're trying to pull a fast one. You've got a better chance of keeping the old sot in line than anybody else in town since he seems to like you."

"Chief, no one can keep that man in line."

Richards let out a deep sigh. "You'd better. It's your job." The chief dropped the letter, wrapped one hand around a fist, planted his elbows on the desk, and put his hands to his mouth. He wanted to nibble on a knuckle, but he refrained. "Go collect him and bring him in, and we'll see if the two of us can't get him to see reason."

"Chief, is it all right if I wait until after the lunch crowd has cleared out of Club 250? Getting him to come in to see you will be a whole lot easier if he doesn't have a full house to play to."

"Good point," the chief agreed.

* * *

When Lyndon opened the door for Jimmy to enter the chief's office, the old sot belligerently demanded, "What do you want this time?"

"We need to talk about Bremen," the chief said.

"That's settled," Jimmy grumped. "I've already told the boys that the trip is off."

"Dory's in the hospital," the chief said. "She won't be able to travel for two or three months."

"So?" Jimmy asked.

"The trip is scheduled for right after the Fourth of July. Magdeburg is insisting that we stick to the plan. With Asa and Dory out of the picture, Magdeburg wants you to make the trip as the representative of Clan McDonald."

"Hello? The name is James Richard Shaver. Not McDonald."

"Yes. But since you're listed in that Berlin Philosophical Quarterly as the war chief for the local clan McDonald, and with Laird Asa not going, Magdeburg says you need to."

"What? First, you tell me I can't go. And now you're telling me I have to go?"

"That's about it, Jimmy. Someone from Clan McDonald of Grantville has to be in Bremen in July or there will be diplomatic hell to pay."

"Chief, the point was to take *Dory*."

The chief nodded. "She can go anytime she wants to. We just need someone to go in July to put an end to the idea that Clan McDonald is planning on conquering a kingdom. That's your fault. So you get to go."

"Without Dory, I ain't interested."

"That doesn't matter." The chief put both palms flat on the desktop and stared back at Jimmy, who was standing in front of the desk, Lyndon behind him. "Magdeburg wants an end to all the wild stories that are causing no end of problems."

"You need some McDonalds. Shoot, chief, even with a bagpipe and a kilt, no one is going to believe that I'm a McDonald."

The chief raised his eyebrows. "Jimmy, weren't you listening? The Berlin Philosophical Quarterly has published a letter telling all of Europe that you are the war leader for the local McDonalds. But a bagpiper is a good idea. And I know where we can get one. Come to think of it, I think you've got two or three of them to make the trip with you. And I'm sending Lyndon along to keep you out of trouble."

"You're putting me on, right?"

The chief solemnly shook his head.

"You want me to lead a team of bagpipers to Bremen to look at a statue of a chicken, on a cat, on a dog, on a donkey?"

"Yes."

"Chief, I'll admit it. You can make me go. But if you think for one minute that you are going to get me to wear a kilt, you had better think again."

"Then, you'll do it?" The chief asked.

"Have I got a choice?" Jimmy replied.

"No. Not really."

Artists From Afar
John R. Deakins

This story is the sequel to "Chiaroscuro" in Grantville Gazette 89

1635

It always seemed to be damp in Venice. Giorgio Fabrini, the former Father Benedetto, clambered from the gondola. The boat's rocking would have bothered anyone new to the city, but he was sufficiently used to it. He climbed the stairs to the rooms he shared with his wife Mirabella and baby Antonio. She greeted him at the door with a kiss, her dark hair swirling around her shoulders.

"How was it today?"

"Much the same as any other day. I'm a much better engraver than I was two or three years ago, but Master Ronelli has me slogging through the same mundane, ordinary work as any apprentice. I've done more landscape backgrounds than any engraver in Venice, I think. I'm not some snot-nosed fifteen-year-old, but you couldn't tell it by the way he treats me.

"I worked in Molise, and I became a better engraver. I worked in Abruzzi, and became better still. I worked as a scribe in Ancona and Urbino, but I didn't want to stay in the Papal States. We picked up enough money, and we moved on. We used our money to get through Romana and Bologna, and we barely paused in Ferrara. I was so sure that Venice would be different." He frowned. "Very well. Oh, I suppose it is.

"Here, we're almost beyond the civil war between the two Popes. There are plenty of opportunities for a scribe, a translator, or an engraver. I just had the bad luck to choose the wrong master. Master Ronelli is touchy. If I leave him and try to get work with another engraver, he'll blacklist me with every engraver in town. It would take him longer to cause me trouble if I tried to work as a scribe or found work translating English. There's plenty of documents that come out of that Grantville place that need to be transferred to Italian or Latin. None of that would matter if I got Ronelli angry with me. He has plenty of connections with the other Venice merchants. I have to keep working for him as long as we're here—but I have some good news.

"I've saved enough money for us to move on. With my salary and the small amount your father had put by, we can buy another donkey, maybe a younger one this time. We'll hitch him to our cart, load everything, and be on our way to Austria, over the Alps before this year's summer ends. There'll be enough travelers so that we won't be alone. Less fear of bandits that way. I've already worked out the route that we'll take to the Low Countries." She didn't rush forward with enthusiasm to embrace him.

"You seem to have forgotten something. I was pregnant when we got to Abruzzi. The old donkey died, and the baby was born. All you could think about was buying another old donkey and moving on. You've dragged me and Antonio half the length of Italy, just to get to Venice. All right. So you could have gotten in trouble with one Pope or the other. So what?

We've been sick half the time since we've been here. I won't mind leaving Venice much, but must we leave Italy? In Austria, I won't be able to speak to anyone. We could go to Florence, or Milan, or Genoa."

"We won't be staying in Austria. I plan to go on to Munich, in Bavaria. Then on to Stuttgart, and—"

"What? More countries full of foreigners? Are you some kind of migrating bird who must fly on and on? Are you some butterfly, fluttering from country to country, like a bug from flower to flower? What if I don't want to travel to all those places?" Her dark eyes flashed. She'd been a country girl from a small town in the Apennines all her life. She'd already spent all the time on the road that she wanted. Nevertheless, he'd been prepared for her reaction.

"We need to sell your father's paintings. They're Antonio's legacy. That will be the money that establishes our family. I'd think that as a dutiful wife and mother you'd see that." Knowing his beautiful, but stubborn, wife, Giorgio had prepared, and he didn't intend to be entirely fair in his arguments. She looked stricken.

"We could sell those paintings in Florence or Milan or—"

"Not with the way things are. In Italy, there won't be any more religious art purchased until it's clear that there's one Pope and one Pope only. We have to get to the other side of the Alps to find a buyer, or Antonio's stake in life will be cut to half or less."

"Perhaps as far as Austria then—"

"Part of my treasure is that American pamphlet, the piece of one of their *encyclopedias* that told me about Caravaggio. I know that you never knew your father by that name, but in the world of art, that name still carries power. The article said that Peter Paul Rubens was strongly influenced by Caravaggio. I've been listening, and I've heard about his fame as an artist, and about his wealth. That man will give us the true value for your father's paintings. We can use the money to establish ourselves among the Flemish." He fired a quick prayer of thankfulness to Heaven. His wife had no more idea how far away the Low Countries were from Venice than she knew about the back side of the Moon.

"You and your fixation on Grantville! If the Americans are so wonderful, why aren't you determined to go *there*?"

"I told you: I've been listening. The Americans have many things, but they don't seem to have any inclination to pay large amounts for paintings. Antwerp, where Rubens lives, has become one of the great artistic centers on the continent. I also hear that the Netherlands is now a stable country. We could probably gain as much money for the paintings in Madrid or Paris, but the talk tells me there will be another war not far in the future. Those countries will be involved, but they'll be fighting the Americans. Every source I have says the same thing. The Americans are almost miraculous in their powers. King Fernando and the Netherlands are American friends. France and Spain will do nothing except lose to them. I plan for our family to be established, with money, living on the winning side in such a war."

Giorgio then played his last, strongest card. He took Mirabella in his arms and kissed her soundly. They'd only been married a little more than a year. The *newlywed* fire in their bodies still burned hot. She caught fire from his excitement. In a few moments, he had Mirabella out of her Italian peasant's blouse, kissing her ample Italian breasts, and then out of all her clothing. In little more time, they were fully entwined on the room's narrow bed, with baby Antonio watching from across the room. Giorgio had lived as a priest, with many years of celibacy to make up for. Mirabella found herself thoroughly *convinced*. In fact, he was able to convince her twice more that same evening.

Within a week, they were on their way across the mountains. They traveled quickly and quietly from Tyrol, through unstable Bavaria, before the winter arrived. Fleeing from Austria, with the threat of the Ottomans looming on the southeastern horizon, was an idea that had occurred to many Austrians. The Italians were never alone on the road, and peasant refugees with a donkey cart attracted no particular attention. They were able to rent a tiny apartment in Stuttgart, in a building crowded with other immigrants.

During the cold months, Antonio died of pneumonia after a week of fever. In the spring, Mirabella was notably pregnant again. Only that prevented her from sinking into hatred for her husband. She would forever consider Giorgio's wanderlust as the cause of Antonio's death, but infant mortality was too common in their century to hold the power that it would someday have in the age of medical miracles.

The new year of 1636 saw them traversing Mannheim and Luxembourg. Giorgio, working occasionally as a scribe, also translated English documents into Latin. That brought him news from churchmen and travelers, so that the pair were able to dodge minor wars. Late in the summer, they entered Belgium and began to ask after the residence of the famous artist.

* * *

"Anthony, my friend! Do come in." The servant who'd been escorting the younger man, as was his function, bowed out of the room. Anthony van Dyck approached the seated figure by the fireplace. Just arrived from a brisk summer day, the younger painter found the room exceptionally warm. He knew from experience, however, that Peter Paul Rubens never failed to have a blazing fire in every room that he inhabited for any length of time. That probably harked back to his childhood poverty. His mother had struggled constantly to maintain the family, with his disgraced father absent. The Rubens family were certain to have been cold more often than they'd been warm.

"Do be seated, my friend. You must tell me the latest news from England." Van Dyck settled into a comfortable chair, moving his torso from side to side, discovering the furniture's superiority.

"Did you design these chairs yourself? I thought you'd given up furniture design decades ago." As Rubens' former journeyman, he'd associated with the great painter for years.

"Oh, I did design these, in a way. My designs have been copied so many times in so many countries that I long since gave up trying to control my furniture creations. The Americans are the only ones who pay attention to patents. These were crafted by a talented furniture maker in Brussels." Rubens rang a silver bell on the table beside him. The dutiful servant appeared instantly. "Wine for my guest. Make it a good vintage. Dilute mine with two parts water. Bring a tray of brown bread and cheeses, as well." He turned to the man who'd once been his protégé.

"How was the journey?"

"You know well that travel is only something a man endures. A ship from Dover to Antwerp is one of the least miserable ways to move about."

"When will you be returning to England?"

"If I can find a way, I probably won't be returning at all. Things are not as they once were."

"Oh?"

Van Dyck pursed his lips, as if reluctant to answer, but then he relaxed. "I know that you've always gotten on well with King Charles, as have I. I'd have spent the rest of my life in England. You know what those strange *histories* say, the ones that the Americans brought from the future. In two more years, I was to have married a queen's lady-in-waiting." He shook his head.

"The queen is dead, and that's addled the king's mind. That damned Richelieu waved those *histories* under Charles' nose, until he could manipulate England like a toy. Charles sold the French all of his New World possessions for a handful of gold and a kiss on the bum. I care nothing about that, but that has to have been a foolish move. You've seen the maps. There's more territory across the water than every country we've ever visited. Then, Charles turned on the Dutch, a dastardly thing to do.

"But that's not the worst of it. Richelieu made sure that the king saw all the passages about the coming rebellion against him. He's gone through all England, arresting people who'd someday rebel against him. Their families have been killed or imprisoned, for no reason. Time and again, loyal noblemen have been thrown into the Tower or executed. He sees enemies behind every bush. You remember those excellent portraits I painted of him? Not long before I left, I painted another one. Of course it flatters him. He *is* the king after all. I wouldn't do anything less.

"I had to take great care with what I produced. His face is gaunt. His beard, which had formerly been neat and pointed, is ragged and untrimmed. He's become afraid of barbers, because of the razors they use. His eyes are full of madness and fear. I had to be careful not to paint that. I won't be returning within his reach if I can help it. Next week or next month, he might decide that I was conspiring against him. Since those Americans escaped the Tower with Cromwell, the warders there have become cruel and suspicious. I fear to see the inside of that place." Van Dyck stared at his feet, shaking his head like a man trying to negate evil changes in his universe. Rubens shook his head in empathy.

He sighed. "I believe that you'll like the Low Countries better. Business is growing again. The artists and craftsmen have returned to Antwerp. Fernando is king of all now, but the Netherlands has made it plain that they'd go to war again in a second if he tried to roll back the freedoms that they gained. If he tried anything foolish, he'd have to put down a rebellion among the Flemish, also, I think. You're welcome to be my guest as long as you wish. This place is huge."

Van Dyck smiled. "I've heard how well you're doing. Some say that Peter Paul Rubens never met a golden guilder that he didn't like." Rubens barely smiled. "Ah, the same old Master, a solid Dutchman who never laughs at himself. Look at the way you dress. You don't look at all like the greatest artist that Antwerp has ever produced. You look like a cloth merchant or a banker, and not a rich banker at that. From what I've heard, you own half of Flanders."

Van Dyck smiled again. "Oh, don't be so sour! You tower above everyone in this state. Everything you ever put your hand to was a success. Any other Fleming would be enjoying his retirement, but you're still painting like the master you've always been. There's not a diplomat in Europe who's more in demand."

Rubens sighed again. "No matter how you wrap it, my rheumatism simply won't let me do what I was once able to do. I don't have the stamina anymore." Van Dyck laughed aloud.

"No stamina? I hardly think so. You've married a beautiful sixteen-year-old girl, when a man your age should rightfully be dead, at least from the belt down. You've fathered four children. You've turned out more masterwork paintings than any painter alive. You're still a noted diplomat, even if you say you don't want to travel that road anymore. You've designed furniture and engravings. You have one of the greatest, best-maintained art collections in Europe. I hear that every day you take one of your spirited horses out for a one-hour ride. You'll soon be sixty, but you insist on showing up the rest of us."

That time Rubens did smile fully. He was a man who recognized his own greatness, part of which was to seek ever higher achievements. "Your very praise shows any greatness that I might have to be a fraud. I may be between diplomatic missions, but that's no excuse for bad manners. You, of all men, are one of the best living persons who can appreciate my collection; yet, I haven't shown it to you. You've justly praised my beautiful wife; yet I've failed to introduce her to you. You've used my children as an example of my stamina; yet, I've failed to present them to you. Bring your wine, Anthony, and come view my collection with me."

Rubens had moved to his renovated castle-mansion, Steen, as much for extra space as anything. Certainly it was luxurious, but his mansion in Antwerp had been the same. Steen was larger than his city dwelling had been. It had to be. His art collection had been about to squeeze his family and guests out. Steen's long halls and multiple chambers now housed innumerable Greek and Roman marbles, tapestries, and the finest paintings in all Europe, including some of Rubens', which he'd kept instead of selling. Van Dyck was flattered to find a half-dozen of his own works scattered through the mansion's hallways.

Van Dyck, who'd been intimate with kings and nobles, was nevertheless overwhelmed by the volume of magnificent art. The Italian masters alone were worth untold thousands. With his head still spinning, Van Dyck, with Rubens, came finally to a magnificent dining hall. A richly dressed woman met them there, servants hovering in the background.

"Anthony, may I present to you my wife, Helene Fourment-Rubens."

Lady Rubens indeed had a beautiful face, and van Dyck could tell from the way that her husband's eyes never left her that the great artist was still very much in love. Too much good food and rich living, however, had expanded her figure from voluptuous to Junoesque. She was at least twice the woman that Rubens had first married.

"Meneer van Dyck, I am most pleased to meet you. I never met you in the past, but the fame of your special beard precedes you. Peter Paul has often spoken well of you. You will, of course, be our guest for dinner this evening and plan to stay for an extended visit."

"I would be most delighted, madam."

Rubens quirked one corner of his mouth. "You'll be astounded at the quality of table that Helene will present to you this evening," Rubens said. "Her last banquet was fifteen courses. She's the consummate mistress of our great house." Madame Rubens cast her eyes downward.

" Peter Paul flatters me now, but watch as he eats tonight. My husband only touches bread and cheese, or raw vegetables, with a little watered wine."

"My darling, you know what Lady Jefferson said before she left for New Amsterdam."

She sniffed. "I care not how elevated the knowledge of those Americans is, if it's going to ruin the perfectly good meal I've planned." She sniffed again.

"My dear Lady Rubens," van Dyck offered, "when I was an apprentice in his studio, many years ago, that's all he ate then as well. Be not offended by his simple appetite. Even to the eyes of a stranger, his love for you is manifest." The younger artist bowed and kissed her hand. The sound of a man's social stock rising makes no noise, or the trio would have been deafened. Rubens kissed his wife's cheek and gave her a brief hug.

"I'll be with the children at my usual time this evening. Let's give Anthony a chance to rest before dinner. He's at the end of a long journey." The gentlemen adjourned to Rubens' sitting room again. Rubens called for more wine for his guest, but he barely sipped his own.

"Lady Jefferson warned me that any wine at all could inflame my gout. Look at my hands." He held them where van Dyck could study them in the firelight. The fingers were slightly puffy and reddened.

"You should have seen them three days ago. They're greatly improved. I can paint again. It's lucky that I prefer bread and cheese and good Flemish smoked herring. Those I can have, but there will be no more goose liver, kidney pie, or beef tongue. The list of things I can't eat is far longer than those I can. That's one reason I shouldn't travel on the diplomatic circuit anymore. When a king serves you some dangerously rich dish, you must eat it and smile. You'll have to be the one to do honor to all of Helene's marvelous courses tonight."

"Meneer Rubens, I've read the same 'future' books that you have. We know the dates of our deaths—"

"We do not! When Grantville arrived, everything changed. You yourself told me about the changes that have happened in England. Here, Fernando is king, married to a beautiful queen, whom he never so much as met in that other *history*. I refuse to accept the fact that changes so great can happen to nations, without realizing that they can happen to a single person as well. I hired some researchers to find out about the end of my life. This gouty rheumatism would have killed me four years from now, but I'm not going to let it! My fingers are working, and I'll still be painting when I'm seventy."

Van Dyck failed to smile in agreement. "I don't have gout myself. What will prevent me from dying five years from now, as the American histories say?"

"I saw that same notation, how the *famous* van Dyck died only a year after the *famous* Rubens. I read further. You started some great project in England, but it gave you all kinds of difficulties. You ruined your health, running around trying to solve your problems with that project. Why do you think I wrote to you, to avoid such projects? I well remember how I had to generate one hundred and twelve paintings for King Phillip's hunting lodge that he was converting to a palace. It wore me out completely, and I now regret doing it. That exhaustion moved me one step closer to death, and I didn't want the same thing to happen to you. It's God's own blessing that you've now escaped the land that would have killed you.

"Sometimes those histories were right. I bought Steen because history said that I would. I looked at it, and I liked it. I kept my nephew Phillip as my investment banker, because the history said that he did a good job for me and made me money. On the other hand, I refuse to die on schedule. Oh, I'll someday go down. All of us will. That's God's business, not mine. What I won't do is go down without a fight, not four years from now or whenever. I expect the same from you.

"The histories say that you're an artistic genius, but that your style and my style aren't the same. Fine. Let them not be the same. You're a young man when compared to me. It's been my plan to give you more than the five years you thought you had coming. Formerly, I was too proud to ask you directly to come back to the Low Countries, but I regret that now. I'm especially glad you're here." He waved a hand toward the galleries of paintings.

"While you were looking at the Michelangelos and the Raphaels, I was having a second look at my van Dycks. The books were exactly right. You *do* have a different, unique style, but it has a genius all its own. Anthony, how would you like to make a great deal of money?"

"That's a foolish question. You know how both of us would have answered that question, if it had been asked when we were twenty. Now...that's still a foolish question, since I'm a refugee from my former employment, with no great prospects before me."

Rubens smiled. After all, money was involved. "Anthony—you must call me Peter Paul if we're going to work together again."

"We're going to work together?"

"Probably. Hear me out. Prospective customers ignore my white hair and my need to be near my family. Offers continue to pour in for me to complete some project or other. For every four offers I receive, I have to turn down three. I don't have the time or the strength anymore to complete them all and travel if diplomacy calls me. What I'm painting right now is mostly landscapes from around Steen. I haven't fully explored my potential as a landscape painter yet. I was never a great fan of portrait painting. For all I know, King Fernando may twist my arm to act as his envoy again soon. I've completed more religious works, but my portraits were good enough to generate demand, even today.

"On the other hand, you're probably the best portrait painter in all Europe. Here's my plan. When someone comes to me asking for a portrait, I'll plead age and infirmity. Then, I'll direct them to the extremely talented portrait painter, Anthony van Dyck. You'll take as much gold from them as possible for the portrait, from which I'll get ten percent, as a finder's fee."

Van Dyck blinked several times. "You know I'll need to think about this."

"That's only reasonable. Why not rest for the remainder of the afternoon? I'm sure Helene has had your luggage moved to our best guest-room. She'll send a servant for you when dinner is ready. I recommend against eating anything else in the meantime. You'll want to have plenty of room once you see her table." Rubens rang his bell for the servant. Van Dyck was polite, but thoughtful, with his gratitude, before the servant led him from the room.

* * *

Rubens' personal servant cleared his throat before he interrupted his master's relaxation beside the fire. "Sir, there's a gentleman at the door who wishes to see you. I'm not familiar with him. He's carrying a large, flat parcel—the kind you use to protect paintings. He had no calling card, and he certainly is no noble. He's not armed with a sword."

"It's probably some young man who wishes to become a painter. I'm not in the business of taking on apprentices, but Meneer van Dyck's presence has reminded me that journeymen may grow into masters someday. I'll at least talk to the man, Franz. Send him in."

A young man entered, not yet thirty, carrying his parcel. Rubens didn't rise. He was a master after all, and the young man was a supplicant. His servant remained quietly in the background, prepared, if he was wrong, to conduct a noble interloper to the exit, politely. Similarly, he might have to bodily eject a commoner annoying his master.

"Please introduce yourself, sir."

"My name is Giorgio Fabrini." The newcomer spoke in Latin, oddly accented, as one might who'd traveled extensively. Rubens, a diplomat who'd heard many accents, recognized the voice, name, and clothing as Italian. "What is your business with me, Signor Fabrini? Do you wish to show me some of your work? If your business is mundane, such as furnishings, I'll send you to my butler."

"It's not my work that I wish to show you. I will move it into the light so that your masterful eye can appreciate it fully." He opened the flat package, which had been partially dismantled already. Fabrini pulled a painted canvas free and held it so that the light from the fireplace could strike it fully. Rubens studied it closely. At Rubens' gesture, the newcomer brought it closer to the painter's eyes. The older man stared harder, concentrating.

"Franz, bring that six-branched candlestick. Light a good candle in each socket. I want to see this better." The servant scurried away.

Peter Paul Rubens would have none but the most conscientious of servants. Franz was back in record time with the candles. He lit each with a taper from the fireplace flames. Rubens rose quickly and held the light close to the painting, as if checking each brushstroke. At last, he straightened and looked at Giorgio.

"Do you know what you have here?"

"Yes. Yes, I do. I will not put a name to the picture's painter. You're the master. If I made a claim to the paintings' source, you could either refute it or support it. My word would be nothing. I have seen much great art, but I'm no painter myself."

"Wait. Perhaps it was the accent, but did you imply that you have more than one of such paintings?"

"I did. You are correct. This painter is dead, but his death is recent, not twenty-five years ago."

"I met the man in 1607, but I heard that he died in Porto Ercole and was buried there, not three years later. You haven't—"

"He didn't die then. It was a deception. He's been living under an assumed identity for two decades. He painted during that time, and in reality, he died about two years ago. This isn't the only one of his paintings. I have seven altogether."

Rubens gripped the arms of his upholstered chair and sat down carefully. "Seven? There are seven more Caravaggios that the world has never seen? The man was far ahead of his time. He knew how to show life in a new, more real way. He was rebellious, but I think the power of his art went along with the way he lived his life. With him, it was one more duel, one more pitcher of wine, or one more whore, year after year."

The newcomer looked sad. "That changed, I think. He used to turn out paintings in great numbers. He told me that he once did three in a month. For these last twenty years, he averaged only about one a year. He almost died in 1610, and I think that frightened him. The wife he loved helped settle him down. He was living a very quiet life as a wine-grower."

"A wine-grower? Twenty years—twenty paintings? That's more than seven. Where are the rest?"

"In a shrine to Our Lady of the Walnut, in the mountains of central Italy. Until I arrived there, none had been identified as Caravaggio's work.

The seven I have have never been seen publicly. They didn't come from the shrine."

Rubens was perspiring lightly. "Yes. Yes. God knows how many of my own works grace cathedrals and convents and churches. Until this moment, I hadn't realized how much Caravaggio's work and his attitude had influenced me."

"You may not have known it, but history knew it. I read about his influence on you in a fragment of a book that the Americans brought from the future. In Venice, I also heard you were the greatest art collector in Europe. That's how I knew to bring his paintings to you."

"The Americans? I find their fingers in everything, it seems. Wait. Why is there no mention in those future histories of these lost Caravaggio paintings?"

"I don't know. That shrine was supposed to have burned down once already. Maybe it did burn down before that future history was written. His daughter, my wife, was the only one who knew where he kept his other paintings. She almost died as well. Perhaps everyone who knew where the other paintings were died before the histories were written. There was some money there, in the cave with the paintings, and there were many bandits about; some of them knew about that cave. Someone may have found the money, but left the paintings to rot, not knowing their value.

"I found his paintings because of the Americans, too. I had a fragment of one of their *encyclopedias* with an article about him. There wouldn't be two popes if the Americans hadn't interfered. I'd seen enough of his paintings to recognize them in the shrine, but I only arrived at the shrine to escape the civil war within the Church. Grantville did change *everything*. I see now why so many think that they're angels or demons."

"Incredible! You've left this old man stunned. I would be most interested in buying these paintings from you for my collection. Please, bring the other six here. You know that I will have to verify each one, but I already have faith in their genuine nature.

"Franz! Escort Signor Fabrini to the door, and help him on his way in any way possible. Loan him one of my horses—No, hitch up the carriage instead. He'll need the space for his return journey. Signor Fabrini, it grows late in the day. Bring your family back with you. We have more than enough space for guests, and we will have a banquet this evening. Bring everyone and the paintings back here as quickly as possible.

"Franz, as soon as you have set Signor Fabrini on his way, call Meneer van Dyck, and have him meet me here. Be gentle. He may be sleeping, but he'd never want to miss this." Rubens clapped his hands and shooed the two men from the room.

After the newcomer had left, Rubens noticed that he'd kept possession of the probable Caravaggio. He set it and the candles so that he could get the best possible look at it. He was certain that the younger man would notice that the painting was missing when partway to his destination. As a commoner, however, he wouldn't dare come back and demand it from Rubens. That would imply dishonesty in a nobleman. Certainly, there'd be no problem in the long run, but Fabrini would be painfully nervous about the separation from his property until he was able to return.

Within a few minutes, a rumpled-looking van Dyck arrived at the sitting room. Rubens didn't explain the reason for the summons. He simply waved the other painter over to the new canvas and asked for his opinion. Van Dyck looked at the painting, showing the Egyptian army being drowned by the returning Red Sea.

Van Dyck ran his hands through his disheveled hair. "The colors and the brushstrokes are definitely Italian. I know I've seen that style somewhere. Hmmm. Look at how the pain and fear are etched on the faces of the Egyptian soldiers. You can see their fear clearly as their bodies are thrown into the killer wave's shadow. All is dark under the wave itself, with only the horses and parts of the men emerging into the light. Now, who—? Caravaggio! Certainly, Caravaggio. No one did *chiaroscuro* as well as Caravaggio."

Rubens agreed. "Is it his, or has it been done by some student of his?"

"I never heard of Caravaggio having any students. He was too impatient and unstable for that. He was on the run much of the time, I think. He had more than one order out for his arrest after a dueling opponent died." Van Dyck rubbed his pointy beard.

"What about an imitator?"

Van Dyck decided to withhold judgment. "The brushstrokes would tell us, but I never had the chance to travel much across Italy. I've never seen enough Caravaggios in Genoa to be certain. He was being forgotten when I was in Italy. I know that you were there longer, in more places. What do you think?"

"I think that this is a genuine, unknown painting by Caravaggio. But I fear that, in my excitement, I could make an error. Either this is a Caravaggio, or it's an imitation painted by the most talented imitator I've ever seen. I refuse to make a final decision until the other six arrive."

"There are more? There are *six* more?" Van Dyck's eyes lighted up.

Rubens glanced at his own door. "So I'm told. They should be on their way here now. We'll see. We will just *see*."

* * *

The sitting room was lit by at least twenty candles. Several sets were in portable holders so they could be brought close to the seven paintings. Rubens had ordered seven easels to be brought from his studio, to display the art properly. He continually fluttered from one to the next, like a bee in the richest patch of flowers he'd ever found. His brief comments indicated nothing but approval, nothing but one happy discovery after another.

He'd gone over all seven several times before Anthony van Dyck was able to excuse himself from Lady Rubens' fabulous feast.

Van Dyck smirked. "I think Fabrini is afraid to excuse himself from the dinner, for fear of offending your wife. That might, of course, offend you. He has to have carried all these paintings all the way from Italy. Being separated from them now must be like being separated from your children. His wife is large with child, but her face was thin enough that I doubt that she's been overeating. She blushes constantly, being in the presence of a noblewoman."

Van Dyck quirked one corner of his mouth; "overeating" did belong in the same narrative as Lady Rubens. She'd not only served a dozen courses, but she'd enjoyed each one personally. "What have you concluded? Are they all genuine?"

"I have no reason to believe they aren't. I'll make him an offer for all seven when he finishes the dinner."

"Peter Paul, remember that this is a poor man, from all we can tell. You're a rich man." He waved his hand in a negating fashion toward the great artist. "I know. I know. You didn't get to be a rich man by throwing away your money. Offer him less than they're worth, if you must, but that will still be in the hundreds of guilders. To him and his family, that will seem like an incredible fortune. Nevertheless, I have an idea that will cost you no money, but will seem to be golden to Fabrini.

Van Dyck continued. "I sat next to him during the dinner, and I found out much of his history. He seemed reluctant to talk about what he did before he discovered the paintings, but after their discovery, the man often made his living as an engraver. He reluctantly admitted that he's a very good engraver. That reluctance convinced me. If we can find him a position in Antwerp as an engraver, the price of the paintings will set him and his family up for the rest of their lives. That set me to thinking. Do you remember Vosterman?"

Rubens remained neutral. "Yes. He was probably the best engraver of my works that I ever had. You know, of course, that we parted on less than the best of terms. He moved to England, as you did."

Van Dyck knew Rubens' habits well. "I wasn't there when you parted, but I suspect that the bad terms had to do with money. Think about it. The turmoil that's driven me from England is the same turmoil in which Vosterman is still living."

Rubens waved the comment aside. "The upset was more on his part than it was on mine. Enough years have passed so that I hold the man no animosity. I know the quality of his work, and he'll only have gotten better through experience in London. He returned there, you know, after the American town arrived. Something about that arrival panicked him. Do you know his fate? He was doomed to die blind and in poverty in Antwerp. I was godfather to his son, who's training with him in England. We shouldn't let his death happen! I know that I'm a man known to hold grudges, but I'm also a man who must meet God in only a few years."

Van Dyck was ready to proceed. "Good. What you say is true. I've often used him as the engraver for my own works. Nevertheless, I've now escaped from the insanity around Charles, but Vosterman is still living in it. King Charles still values your work and your reputation. What if you wrote him and requested that Vosterman travel here to assist you with engraving a miniature of Charles' deceased wife, Henrietta Maria? Vosterman would bring a portrait of the late queen, which I painted not long ago. Remember: *you are too old and too infirm to travel to England.*"

Van Dyck smiled at the joke they'd be playing. "You then write a second, private letter to Vosterman, telling him to prepare for his escape. He could quietly send his family ahead. Charles would formerly have paid no attention, but he's suspicious of any artist leaving England. Vosterman would arrive in Antwerp with the best attitude toward you. The two of us can generate all the work he'll want until his reputation is re-established. He'll owe you a favor, and introducing him to a talented new engraver, to become his apprentice, will seem less than nothing for him to grant. The new engraver's presence may save his sight."

Rubens mulled over the proposal for only a few moments. "Anthony, you're a genius. I can only see good coming from this. Anyone with a soul so romantic should indeed have married a queen's lady-in-waiting."

Van Dyck waved off the suggestion. "I'd hardly met the woman. She's comely enough, but if she's really interested in me, perhaps she'll emigrate to Antwerp. Until now, all we had was one of those arranged-at-court rela-tionships. When I'm re-established here, I'm sure that the Low Countries will have a sufficiency of female prospects. Since the Americans came, the events of two years move more rapidly than an entire lifetime of events did before. Did you know? I was once to paint the portrait of Cardinal Richelieu, a dead man"

Rubens found that laughable. "Franz, call Meneer Fabrini from his feast while he can still walk. Prepare to make him an offer."

* * *

Peter Paul Rubens, being the man he was, began with a substantial offer for the paintings far below what they were actually worth. Giorgio Fabrini, an Italian, countered with an asking price far higher than he expected to get. He was intimidated by the presence of two of the world's greatest living painters. That caused him to buckle under negotiating pressure sooner than normal. He quickly dropped his price, as Rubens raised his offer.

They were moving toward a mutually acceptable price, roughly twice what Fabrini could have gotten in Italy, when Rubens suggested that he could acquire Giorgio a position as the engraving apprentice of the elder

Lucas Vosterman. The former priest quickly accepted Rubens' latest monetary offer.

The gold for the paintings was substantial. It would set up his family comfortably in the Netherlands or Antwerp. Nevertheless, the time would come when the gold ran out. Employment as an engraver, with one of Europe's most renowned engravers, was a certified future that would support his wife and child, lighting with income the mists of an unknown future.

He embraced Van Dyck, whose frown had nudged Rubens twice toward a higher offer. He shook hands with Rubens, but bowed to him afterward, not knowing which salutation the great artist preferred. The deal was done. Because that was the real life of the seventeenth century, they all lived happily ever after.

Green, Blue, And Bruises
Natalie Silk

Zaborstadt

Dora shifted the heavy basket on her left arm to be more comfortable and looked over at Anya, her niece—who was obediently standing behind her—before knocking on the simply made door. She tucked a wayward black curl back into her cap just as she heard the door's latch. A six-year-old brown-haired boy with hazel eyes looked up expectantly at his visitors. She gave him a gentle smile with a bit of good-natured amusement. "Good day, young one. May we enter?"

The little boy, with his chest out and mouth set, announced emphatically, "Mama had my baby brother two nights ago."

"Yes, I know. That is why we're calling today."

"Gregor! Let them in." A thin-faced, elderly woman came to the door. She appeared as tired as she sounded, but still managed to smile warmly at Dora and Anya.

"Good day, Beryl."

"Come in. Frau Stein will be back shortly. She was needed at home." Beryl stepped aside. "She knew that you would be visiting."

They allowed their eyes to adjust to the dimness of the small, tidy home.

A woman—who resembled Beryl—and her newborn baby were sleeping in a bed close to the hearth. Just then she stirred with a gentle stretch and opened her eyes to see that she had visitors.

Dora walked to her bedside. "Good day, Sarah, I understand the birthing went well. Very capable hands, Rhea."

"Yes. Yes. She's very good. Zaborstadt is fortunate to have such a wonderful midwife as she."

"This is fine. When will your husband and father return from Grantville?"

"They should be back tomorrow. The baby came early. Quite a surprise."

Dora gave the swaddled newborn a loving smile. "Oh, he's so precious and beautiful—another son! Such a blessing."

Anya stepped forward and stood by her tia. Dora saw a flicker of an expression, a crease of the brow. She had a feeling that her very young niece was wondering how such a wrinkly, tiny face could be seen as beautiful. She recalled that she had thought the same thing before she had her own three children.

"We brought some vegetables and bread." Dora went over to the table and laid the food in a neat pile while Gregor reached up and took a beet to examine. His grandmother gently took the vegetable from his hands and placed it back in the pile.

"Will your parents leave Spain and come to Zaborstadt?" Sarah asked.

Dora felt that familiar, painful heart flutter when she thought of home, her family, and, most recently, her mother. She missed her mother terribly and wished that her husband had the funds so that she could have gone to mourn with her family. She managed to say, "Since my mother's passing, my father is comfortable with my brother and his family and won't be able to travel."

Sarah's exhaustion almost betrayed her: she seemed as if she wanted to say something, but instead said, "Oh, I apologize. I now recall your mother's passing a few months ago. I'm sorry I said such a thing."

Dora hoped her smile was reassuring. "All is well."

In her best German, Anya carefully pronounced each word, "My father will be 'visit'."

Dora turned her head. Her mouth was tight-lipped; her eyes were disapproving. She gave her niece a subtle shake of her head. She didn't want her niece to say anything about a pending visit. She looked back to Sarah, "Yes, my brother-in-law promised in his last letter to us."

"I'm sure you will be very glad when he arrives."

Anya mumbled, "Thank you." She was looking at her feet.

The women exchanged news of ordinary activities and happenings in the market square until it was time for Dora and Anya to leave.

"Thank you for calling. And for the food."

"Yes, thank you," Beryl echoed.

Anya's step slowed after a while on their silent walk to the next visit. "Tia, I'm sorry for speaking." Her aunt continued to look straight ahead. Anya quickened her step to keep pace.

Dora finally said, "The visit was to benefit Sarah, not us. Do you understand?"

"Si, Tia."

She sighed and added, "The truth is that I don't want you to be disappointed again if your papa doesn't keep his promise."

Anya's brow furrowed. "But I'm sure he will!"

They continued in silence until they reached the next home. Dora knocked on the door and said, "Good day, Mira," to the woman, young and well-fed from the season's bounty, who answered.

"Dora! And I see that your niece has joined you." Mira opened the door wider and stepped aside. "Welcome."

Dora spoke very loudly, so that the elderly woman sitting up in a narrow bed could hear. "How are you today, Mother Tanya?!"

Instead of greeting the visitors, the woman looked over their heads.

Mira answered for her mother-in-law, "This seems to be a good day for her."

"This is well." Dora reached in her basket for a bundle of clean handkerchiefs. "I hope my mending is as good as yours," and handed them to her friend.

Mira examined the stitching. "Your work is better than I could do. I've been too busy with all the housework and Mother Tanya to concern myself with the mending that needs to be done."

"I remember how it was when I was newly married."

"Yes."

"I have other mending that I'll do as soon as the weather turns colder."

Mira nodded in appreciation. "I hope it won't be a harsh winter."

"What have you heard in the market?"

Anya remained close by the door, leaving the two women to their conversation. She promised herself that she would be quiet. She looked around and noticed Mother Tanya beckoning her. The woman appeared to be so pleasant and sweet, with a warm smile. She went to the elderly woman's bedside; why wouldn't she? As soon as Anya was by the bed, Mother Tanya's face contorted to the most hateful expression she had ever seen. Before she could return to her place, Mother Tanya pinched her right forearm. She yelped in pain and fright and jumped back out of reach before she could receive another pinch.

The other two women immediately stopped talking. Tia Dora came to her side and Mira took hold of her mother-in-law's shoulder.

"Take your hand away," Tia Dora said. "Let me see."

"Mother Tanya!" Trying to get the elderly woman's attention was no use; she was now vacantly staring at a place by the door. "You shouldn't have done that!" Mira went to Dora, who was comforting Anya. The poor girl was cradling her arm. "I'm sorry. She does that on occasion. It's not out of cruelty. She doesn't know what she does."

"We understand. I have salve that will prevent bruising. I'll apply it as soon as we are home."

* * *

While Anya tended to the chickens, cleaned the coop, and fetched water, Dora was at the hearth, preparing their evening meal . Her thoughts were interrupted when she heard her two daughters exclaim, "Papa! Papa!" even before she could see him on horseback through the open door. He came into view. Deborah and Roza were jumping and clapping in a gleeful dance. Dora smiled.

"Ah, my girls!" He dismounted. "Let me tend to the horse."

He disappeared from her view, and she turned back to the hearth. When Danel came in, Dora looked up. "You tended to the horse so quickly," she said, making it more question than statement.

"Simon is tending to him."

"Of course. How was your day?"

"It was well. We received a new request. A friend of the Fuggers."

"Good." She smiled and went to the table. There was a tension in her husband, and she wondered why. Why have Simon care for the horse when he preferred to do it himself?

Anya came in, carefully carrying a bucket of water so that she wouldn't spill any.

Dora saw Danel scowl as he asked, "What happened to your arm?"

"We called on Mira and Mother Tanya," Dora told him. "Mother Tanya pinched her arm, and I applied salve and a poultice so there wouldn't be a bruise."

"I see. Does it still pain you?"

"No, Tio. Not anymore," she said, emptying the bucket of water.

"Ah!" he exclaimed, and his head jerked up at a thought. He retrieved a letter with a broken seal from his left pocket. "This arrived today. It's from Yeshua." He placed it in Dora's outstretched hand and she went to her stool by the hearth to read it.

"From Papa! What does it say, Tia? Will he arrive early? Shall we go meet him?" Anya watched hopefully.

The letter began by saying that Yeshua's second wife, Constanza, had given him a strong, healthy son. Yeshua continued on about how proud he was of the baby and how blessed he was to have such a wonderful wife. Dora's brow creased when she reached the last passage, finally understanding her husband's tension and unusual behavior. She looked up at her niece and rested her hand on her lap as if the words on the parchment weighed too much.

Danel stood solidly in place as if he was bracing himself. "He will not be coming."

Anya looked down at the floor, asking, "Why?" with a tremble that was uncharacteristic of her, at least of late.

"Your papa doesn't have the resources to do so, and he doesn't want to leave your new brother and Constanza at this time," Dora said gently. "But he asks after you and hopes you are doing well and says that he loves you very much." She paused and then added, "He also is very sorry he can't come to see you."

"Why can't someone help Constanza? She has family," Anya pleaded.

"Yes, well. We don't know the entire situation," Danel offered.

Dora saw that her husband's words didn't help. Her niece's face grew hot and her eyes welled. Holding back tears, she turned and ran out of the house with such a slam of the door that the latch fell in place. Danel walked over and lifted the latch back up.

* * *

Anya ran. It wasn't until she was in the woods and far away from the house that she dropped down under a fir tree and allowed her anger, frustration, grief, and hate to come out in great, anguished tears. Her feelings blamed Constanza for having a baby now. But it occurred to her between spasms that not only was Papa not coming to visit, he didn't mention wanting to bring her home to Spain.

Only when she felt empty did she stand up and brush her skirt. She was ready to go back.

* * *

Danel looked at the door and then his wife. "She will recover."

"Allow me to care for matters of the heart—and with Anya."

"Extra chores will relieve her mind." Before Dora could respond, he turned his back to her fury and said, "I must tend to my evening prayers."

"When it's a convenience for you!" she cried.

He prayed louder. He could hear her chopping vegetables at the table even over his prayers. Then the chopping stopped. He turned around and saw his wife scowling, standing with her arms crossed. His prayers must end.

"Listen to me," Dora said. "We will go to town. Our entire family for the day. We shall say the purpose is to purchase material at Meller's for a

new shift and skirt for our niece. And we shall find the funds to do so."
Her piece said, she went to her chopping board and continued cutting
vegetables.

"Why must all of us go?"

"*We* are Anya's family. We shall show her that she belongs to us. It is our
duty now to find her a good husband. Truly, her own father doesn't have
any thought for Anya…That cruel man mentioned his daughter only in the
last sentence." Dora added in an exaggerated and sarcastic tone, "'Tell her
that I love her.' Hah!" She emphasized each word with a chop. The poor
carrot didn't have a chance under her blade.

"Dora, my brother is just being protective of his wife and only son, who
is newly born."

"Your nephew is now two months old. Anya is correct to say that family
can help. Yeshua has no concern about leaving his wife and child for
business. He didn't even care to send funds for Anya. Again."

Danel was about to reply when they heard noise on the other side of
the door—two snuffles. They stopped talking. The door swung open, and
Anya stepped over the threshold, giving her right eye a quick swipe with the
heel of her hand. And allowed one more snuffle before composing herself.

Anya rubbed the bandage on her arm. She wanted to feel the pain of the
pinch again and didn't care if her rubbing caused an ugly bruise. "Did Papa
really say all that about me in the letter?" She had to ask even when, deep
down, she already knew the truth.

Dora put down the knife and wiped her hands on her apron before she
came to Anya. "Of course he did." Anya's stomach twinged at the lie. "Your
tio has a grand idea, Anya. He was thinking of taking all of us into town.
We shall go to Meller's Mercantile and Textile Shop for the material and
notions we need. You've outgrown what you have now, and I don't think

I'll add another grow strip. Wouldn't such an excursion be just the thing, Tio?" Dora looked squarely at her husband.

Anya turned her head and saw him swallow before answering. "Yes. Most certainly. It will do us all well."

She could tell it wasn't fully his idea, but that he had agreed to appease her tia. She knew that he didn't want to disagree or argue, only to spend the night in the barn, considering it might rain and be cold.

*　*　*

Simon and the girls were yards ahead of Danel and Dora on the main road to town. Danel was in deep contemplation about all the tasks he had left to his foreman today.

Dora laced her hand in his arm, interrupting his thoughts. "Husband, we'll make do. I was thinking last night." His arm stiffened and he clenched his jaw. "We'll find a good young man for Anya."

Danel stared at her. "She's too high-spirited for the young men in Zaborstadt."

"That can't be true. It may be from being heartbroken. Her papa isn't coming to visit."

Danel shook his head. "I don't think it's just that."

They continued walking in silence, watching Anya follow Simon, Roza, and Deborah into town.

As they neared the Mercantile, Danel spoke again. "I'll come with you. I would like to help. Perhaps you can tell me what dry goods you may need."

"Truly, husband?" Dora looked at him doubtfully. "There's really no need. I'm not liberal with purchases."

"Then let me carry the parcels."

She paused to consider this. "Very well."

In front of the store, a small crowd of children and adults were laughing at a traveling marionette show.

"I can remember as a boy how enjoyable these amusements were!" Danel smiled.

At the same time, Roza pointed at the "theater" and jumped up and down in excitement. "Oh! Let us go see! Please, let us go see!"

"A wonderful idea!" Without hesitating, Danel slipped Dora's hand from his arm and led his children to the brightly painted little theater and the laughing and clapping audience.

"Of course, you will, husband mine," she said under her breath, but he heard her and turned back to see her smiling. Then to her niece, she said, "Come, Anya. We'll let the children be." Anya looked from her aunt to her uncle and giggled at the jest.

Anya followed Dora into the store. Once inside, her aunt directed her to a counter. "The textiles are over there."

Just then Tovah—the blacksmith's wife—entered the store. "Dora!"

Dora straightened and gave Tovah a warm smile. Tovah, always so sweet, pleasant, and forgiving, even after that terrible incident when Dora's two daughters wandered off to town.

Anya stood next to a crate waiting for her tia. She went to the counter alone when she realized the two women were too engrossed in their conversation to end it any time soon. Two bolts of fabric lay on the counter. Her fingers ran softly along the first one, a very beautiful green material that shined. She remembered Mama wearing a gown made of this luxurious-type of fabric. It had also been green embroidered with silver thread. She remembered Mama smiling and turning around so that Papa could admire her. She was told often that with her light brown hair and eyes, she looked like her mother.

Papa smiled broadly, so pleased. Anya ran up to him and threw her arms around his waist in an enthusiastic hug, as much as her small arms could give. "Papa, I want a pretty dress too! Just like Mama's!" "Ah, my dar-

ling daughter," he said, hugging her back, "Someday. Someday you shall."
"Promise?" "I promise." She looked at Mama. "Then I'll be as beautiful as
you." Her mother gave her the smile that she so cherished and loved. "Anya,
you are already beautiful."

Anya touched the second bolt of fabric. It was blue and coarser than the green one, although the fabric could make a fine gown.

"It came from Grantville." A young woman with auburn hair and brown eyes replaced a jar on a shelf, then approached the counter where Anya stood. "Both came from Grantville Fabrics and Textiles. Imagine. A store solely for the purpose of fabrics and notions."

"Truly?" Anya had so many questions. If only her German was better.

"Oh, yes. My mother and father were there last week. This fabric," she said as she lightly touched the green cloth, "came from Tyrol and then to Grantville. It's a remnant from a special gown for a young woman from Grantville who went to Tyrol to teach." Then she touched the blue cloth. "And this one was supposed to be for a nurse to wear while going about her work."

"Nurse?" Anya repeated the strange-sounding word, allowing the sounds to form in her mouth.

"Yes, there are women who learn such skills in Grantville, I've heard. I find it hard to believe such a thing! I'm sure as soon as they become proper wives, they leave that employ."

Anya followed along as best she could, but the young woman was speaking quickly. Anya recalled how she cared for Manuel after he was stung so badly. Then she heard something about money. She grasped for the words she needed to ask. *They are paid wages?* She asked instead, "They get coins?"

"Oh, you mean, do they get paid?" She appeared satisfied that she understood the translations, "Well, of course."

That's what Anya wanted. To go to Grantville! To be a nurse! To have her own money!

Another woman came to the counter. "Jael, please return the fabrics."

"Yes, Mother."

"I've seen you in synagogue before," Jael's mother said. "You must be Anya. Danel and Dora's niece."

Anya gave a bashful smile and shallow, quick curtsy while looking down, just as her aunt and Tovah approached the counter. "Good day, Hannah," they said to Jael's mother.

"Good day. How may I help you?"

"Have your needles arrived?" asked Tovah.

"Yes, two days ago." Hannah pulled a wooden box with lamb's wool and needles from under the counter.

Tovah looked at the selection and retrieved a strip of fabric from her basket. She pulled four of the needles out of the box and inserted them in her strip of cloth. "These will be fine." She carefully placed the strip of cloth and four needles back into her basket before paying for her purchase. "Good day, Hannah. Dora." She was about to turn to leave, but added with a warm smile, "I hope to see you both soon."

"Good day," they both said in turn.

Then, remembering, Tovah added, "And Anya."

Anya curtsied.

After Tovah left, Dora said, "We're here for cloth for a skirt and shift."

"Tia, I like the green cloth that was here."

"Hmm." Hannah looked doubtful. "I don't think that selection will be sturdy enough for everyday wear. And it's rather costly, I must add."

"There was blue cloth. I liked that also."

"Oh, yes. The blue cloth. It was meant—," Hannah searched for the correct words, "for a uniform for a nurse in Grantville."

"Uniform for a nurse? What is this?" Dora asked.

"My husband and I visited Grantville. So many wondrous things to see! There's a school to teach all manner of subjects, including the healing arts." She stopped, her expression searching for something important. "Ah." Her face relaxed. "The healing arts are also taught at the University of Jena." Satisfied, she continued. "My husband and I thought it would be good to send our son to Jena. We discovered much. Ah, yes." She nodded. "Once students learn the skills they need, they practice them under the direction of doctors. They wear uniforms, dresses and aprons for the women, so that people know they are nurses. There is a special place in Grantville for the ill and infirm: a *hospital*. I have to tell you,"—she leaned forward—"there are now places called *clinics* in other towns that also serve the ill and infirm. These places are much smaller than a hospital." Hannah took a step back and turned her head to the right. "Jael! Please come and help! Ach," she said now to Dora and Anya, "That girl. If only for a son." Then more loudly, "Bring the nurse cloth and white linen."

"I just put it away, Mama!" Jael yelled from the back room.

"Jael, the nurse cloth!" Then again to Dora and Anya, "It's a pity we don't have such a clinic here in Zaborstadt."

Dora disagreed. "We have a midwife and there are good wives who know how to care for the ill."

"Yes, this is true. Yet, having a clinic would add to our comfort."

Anya thought about what Hannah said. Going to learn in Jena didn't appeal to her as did Grantville. She had heard so many wonderful stories about Grantville. Surely it was the place for her.

Dora and Anya stepped outside, juggling packages and trying to shield their eyes from the bright sunlight. "Where have your tio and your cousins gone?" The traveling theater had moved from its spot. Looking around, they saw Danel coming down the street. He was holding a cloth bag while

Roza, Simon, and then Deborah took turns in retrieving something from it. They were smiling and eating enthusiastically.

"Ah, my children. What is this you're enjoying?"

"It's been a long time since we indulged in sweets." Danel held the bag out to Anya and then to Dora. "It's not as good as up-time chocolate, but these sweets are just as fine."

"Chocolate?" Dora asked. "When did you have that? We can't afford such a thing."

"The same day I came home with a broken wagon wheel."

"Hmm. *That* I remember."

Danel handed the almost empty bag to Simon. "Share with your sisters." The boy ran ahead with his new-found bounty, Roza and Deborah close behind. Danel sighed in exasperation. "I better go after them."

Anya followed with her aunt. After a while, she said, "I would like to go to Grantville and learn the nursing arts."

Dora stopped walking and turned to her niece, "What is it you say?"

"I want to go to Grantville and learn to be a nurse."

"Your papa will not agree to this. Don't you want to be a wife? If it's the healing arts you want to learn, I can teach you everything I know."

"Tia, I want to be a nurse and have my own money." She took a breath. "Money enough for a suitable man to court me."

"Do you think a suitable man would court a young woman who earns money? Such a thing doesn't exist."

Dora didn't say anything else but she thought about what Anya asked. On the one hand, Yeshua's letters were infrequent and when they did receive one, he hardly mentioned his daughter, much less sent funds, however meager, for Anya's keep. Dora now doubted Anya's father had even set aside funds for a dowry.

"You do understand that you will care for the ill and decrepit such as Mother Tanya." Would this change her mind?

Anya looked straight ahead with a firm and solemn expression. "Si, Tia," she said, quickly looking at her pinched arm and then straight ahead again, "I understand."

"Very well, I'll discuss this with your tio. But I will not promise a good outcome." Dora suddenly stopped. "Learn all you're able to, from me. I'll approach Rhea, the midwife, so that you may continue your training. Are we agreed?"

"Si. But, if I prove myself a capable midwife, may I go to Grantville?"

Dora didn't reply.

* * *

It was a rare moment when Dora was alone with her husband and she took advantage of it. They both sat at the table. "Your brother's daughter wants to go to Grantville and learn to be a nurse."

"Yeshua will never allow this. She's from a prosperous and good family." Dora knew when he gave his beard a single stroke, it was his way of pausing before speaking. "Anya is quite innocent. Grantville may have enticements, but it's not a place for her. She needs to be married."

"This is true, I agree that she should be married. Does your brother have a dowry for her? If he doesn't provide, do we have the funds? When was the last time we received money for her keep? Do you think Yeshua has chosen a suitable young man for her? I would wager that he hasn't given it a thought."

He looked down, contemplating.

She was too impatient for her husband to answer. Sometimes the man could be unfathomably slow. "Humph. I have an idea. *I'll* teach her what I know and she will continue to accompany me during my convalescing visits, while *you* find a good husband for her. Of course." For now, she would keep her other idea to herself.

Danel looked directly at her. "Of course. I'm sure once there is a *kiddushin*, she'll see nursing is folly. I must write to my brother."

"No need to write to Yeshua yet." She hoped the way she smiled conveyed that he should understand what he should do. "But please find a husband for her to begin the betrothal."

* * *

Dora looked for Rhea after the Shabbot service, but found she was meeting with the Rabbi Samuel and his wife Esther. This knowledge refreshed Dora's envy, quickly stifled, of Esther's ability to discuss learned matters with the Rabbi and his students. She did allow herself an inner sigh, knowing she should be grateful that her father had taught her to read and write.

Unable to talk to Rhea at the synagogue, Dora planned to seek her out on the following market day. While walking to market, Dora rehearsed what she would ask Rhea, continuing to mull over the words and just how she would say them, even when she reached town. The streets were crowded in spite of the sky being overcast and looking like rain. A few people haggled over the best prices of goods; others stopped long enough to discuss the news of the day, while small children ran around and through their elders and the stalls, playing a game of touch.

Amid the chaos, she spotted Rhea intent on getting the best price for her selection of fish. Dora took a deep breath and purposefully walked toward the fishmonger, still rehearsing "Rhea—" *Why that little—!* A boy not much older than her Simon was reaching into Rhea's basket while he casually looked around. Dora quickly closed the gap and grabbed the boy's left ear roughly. "*What* do you think you're doing?!"

Rhea and the fishmonger stopped talking to watch, along with nearby people.

"You little thief!" She tugged his ear again for emphasis. He held her arm, yelping in protest, trying to free himself. "You rapscallion!" She shook the struggling boy again.

He continued his yelping, still trying to pry her away from his reddening left ear. "Wha'?! Wha'? Ow! Not me! I'm not doing nothing!"

A man, part of the merchant class by the quality of his clothes, pushed through the small crowd. "What's all this about?"

Dora still had a firm grip on the boy's ear. "He was going to steal from this good woman!" When the man looked at her blankly, she realized that she was speaking Spanish. She repeated herself in German. Rhea and the other women in the small crowd held their baskets closer and a few even checked in them, making sure all their purchases were there. Two men checked for their coin purses.

She pulled the boy closer to the man. "Is he yours?"

The man put his hands on his hips. "He most certainly is not."

"Le' go! Owwww!!"

"Well, this—!" She pulled the boy to her, forcing him to face her. "This—Shame!" Ear tug. "Shame!"

"Le' go! Stop!"

Decisively, the merchant said, "I'll call the watch."

"No! No! I promise not to do it no more!" Dora gave the boy's ear another tug.

Onlookers pointed, chuckled, and nodded at the sight. Others commented on the time that Dora had run through the town brandishing a knife, looking for her missing daughters. What a sight *that* had been!

A man as shabbily dressed as the boy-thief made his way through the growing crowd. Dora suspected that he was the father by his concern for the boy and their shared shape of eyes and mouth.

"Hand over my son!"

"Oh, so this is *your* little thief! Did you teach him everything you know?"

"What?!" He was about to say something else but then quickly said, "No. Never a thief!"

"Papa! Help!"

Dora shook him. "Quiet, you! But he is! I saw him try to steal from this good woman!" She nodded her head towards Rhea for emphasis. Rhea held her basket even closer for emphasis and glared at the man, disgusted.

"I'll take hold of him." He reached for the boy, whose left ear's ugly shade of red surpassed the ruddiness that managed to seep through the grime on his face.

"Papa! I didn' do nothing."

Dora relented, and with a final tug released the youngster into the dirty hands of his father. The father roughly grabbed his son and quickly left the laughing crowd. Dora thought it was the boy's good fortune that the watch hadn't arrived. She said, "Hmmph," to their departing backs.

Rhea approached her. "How many ears do you have in your basket?"

Dora smiled. "Not enough to satisfy."

"Well then, I'm indebted to you. Although I've only begun my market day—meager as it shall be." She patted the side of her basket.

At the mention of being "indebted," Dora had two thoughts: *What if her request was too bold* and *what if all this seemed to be plotted*? She decided to risk it anyway and took a step closer to Rhea.

"I would like to talk to you about my niece, Anya."

"Is she well?"

"Yes, yes of course."

"This is good. Anya and I spoke during services last week."

"Oh?" She said as casually as she was able, even though her mind raced. Was it when the girl had got up for a moment?

Rhea smiled, patting Dora's hand. "My husband told me you wanted to speak to me." Dora almost sighed in relief, until Rhea followed with, "And others came to me and told me how you and your husband wanted Anya to learn the midwifery arts. Of course, I'll teach her. She'll learn much from me. My own Rahel is already quite knowledgeable."

Dora was both glad and embarrassed at how quickly word got around. She thought Rhea was going to decline. "Thank you."

"Tell me, why do you want her to learn midwifery? Is it her desire?"

"Yes, it *is* her desire."

"Truly? I understand that going to Grantville to learn nursing is more to her liking."

It shouldn't have surprised her that everyone would know the happenings in such a small community. Dora swallowed. It was time for her to be honest. "It is our desire that she remain here in Zaborstadt and marry. Grantville is not for her. If she learns midwifery, then all the better. She will have the respect of our rabbi and his council, as well as the synagogue." Dora couldn't admit out loud that she had gotten used to the extra help with the never-ending chores around the home.

"Very well. I'll teach her the skills."

* * *

"It's such good fortune that you will be able to help me with this birth. Rahel has assisted me with two already." Rhea proudly smiled at her daughter and she returned the smile. By the way Rahel was beaming, Anya wondered if the girl received any praise at all from her mother. "Even more fortunate that it's here in our town."

Anya quietly stood back from the midwife and her daughter, not even bothering to hide or stifle a huge yawn. She was truly exhausted from all the chores she had during the day, which included helping her tia with her visits and preparing salves, poultices, and medicines. Although only hours had passed, it seemed like days since she was woken from a deep sleep to join Rhea and Rahel. Why did babies choose to come into the world at night? Anya was sure that learning nursing in Grantville would be easier than this. She had to prove to her tia and tio that she could learn everything they could teach her in Zaborstadt so they would permit her to go to Grantville. She would prove to them that she was capable and deserving to go.

Anya came away from her thoughts when she heard, "—When you and Rahel become midwives, you'll have great respect, as I do. The rabbi and his council will consult you on women's matters." Rhea was scowling at her for not paying attention.

Anya stifled a yawn this time.

Gerda yelled in pain, "My husband! Where is my husband?!" Her moaning increased.

"He's outside."

"I want him *here*!" Gerda cried louder, in another wave of pain.

"He's not permitted, my dear." Then to Anya, "Get more cold cloths for her face and neck," and to Rahel, "We need to walk her again."

Anya went to the wash basin and poured water over the damp cloths. There was another peal from Gerda.

"Good. Back to bed," ordered Rhea.

Once Gerda was settled, the three sat in their chairs around the bed. Waiting. Anya occasionally got up from her place to change the wet cloths on Gerda's neck and face. It kept her from falling asleep in her chair and embarrassing herself. Gerda groaned while Anya applied the cloth to her brow. She swore silently that, if birthing was like this, she did not desire motherhood for herself.

Anya jumped back when Gerda screamed again, loudly. Rhea and her daughter got up from their chairs. Rhea gave instructions to breathe and push while Rahel stood by her mother's side. "Anya, come look. The baby is almost here."

Anya came to Rhea's side. There was a lot of blood. Poor Gerda was screaming and crying. Anya saw the top of the baby's head. Everything turned fuzzy blue, then hazy. Her head hit the floor. She bit her tongue painfully and everything turned black.

Anya felt a hand touch her cheek and then a wet cloth. She slowly and painfully opened her eyes. Her left shoulder and temple hurt. Her tongue hurt. She muffled a groan when Rhea helped her to stand.

Rhea assessed her. "Humph. You have straw on you." She brushed Anya's cheek and neck where they had struck the floor.

Her head cleared enough to recall what had happened. She looked at Gerda who was resting with her swaddled, sleeping newborn, and began to say something.

"A girl," Rahel said. "Her husband will be able to come in now."

Rhea had already surmised what Anya wanted to ask. "It could be from the simple need of sleep that you fainted. My daughter and I needed to help through the pains of birth, and I knew you would be fine until I could attend to you."

"Oh," was all Anya could manage.

"You can help Rahel clean."

She wanted to go home. She wanted the pain to go away. "May I take my leave?"

"After you clean."

Bedraggled and dazed as she was, it took every bit of her remaining strength and will to put one foot in front of another without falling. It was well after dawn when she finally made it home and stumbled over the threshold. She saw Tio and Simon stop eating their thin soup and stare at her. Tia stopped in mid-stride with a bowl for Deborah. Anya's muddled mind allowed her to recall that Roza was asleep in her bed after spending the night tending the hearth. Somewhere in the depth of the moment, she felt a small pang of guilt that she hadn't taken her proper turn and her cousin had to do it in her stead.

"Oh, my. Child, why do you have straw stuck to your skirts? How is Gerda? And the baby? Boy or girl?" Anya only could look at her tia with confusion, her eyes sleep-glazed. The words sounded like a swarm of bees.

When no response came, Dora said, "Wash and eat," and placed the bowl she was holding before Deborah. Her cousin continued to stare at her.

The words "wash" and "eat" pushed through to her.

She mumbled, "I'll wash. But I want to sleep." It was a miracle she made it to her bed. And she slept.

* * *

"Do you think she will lose her desire to go to Grantville and become a nurse?" Danel asked.

She chuckled. "She's stubborn. She should be married with a family of her own."

"I agree. From what I've experienced in Grantville, not all up-timers share our opinion about marriage."

Dora shook her head in dismay and went back to the hearth. She had never been to Grantville, but after the stories she had heard, she believed whole-heartedly that up-time women were wild with strange ideas, and they chose to dress and act shamelessly. "Then up-timers must not worry for their young women." She thought for a moment. "A suitable young man is what Anya needs. She needs to be married and settled before we can properly save for Roza's dowry." Then, with a sigh, "And Deborah's as well."

Deborah looked up from her soup and gave her mother a vegetable-filled smile.

"I'll find such a young man. One who is in a good apprenticeship and from a good family."

"One who knows how to read and write," Dora added.

"Of, course. The true sign of wealth."

***

Dora sat on her stool before the opened door, churning goat's milk to make butter. It was a beautiful day, and she wanted to take advantage of the warmth and light. Newly poured soap lay in a tray beside her. The simple activity of churning butter gave her a chance to daydream. Rhea entered the yard, interrupting an amusing thought. She stopped churning. "Rhea! Good day!" Dora put down the churn and stood up to curtsy.

Rhea curtsied and said, "Good day. I've come for Anya. She's to help me tend to Gerda and the baby."

"Ah, how is Gerda and her baby? A girl? Healthy, I hope."

"Yes, the baby is healthy, and Gerda is doing well."

"That's good."

"Where is Anya?"

"She's inside having her morning meal. She had to tend to the hearth last night."

"I see. I wanted her to join me today to visit Gerda and the baby. Rahel and I visited her yesterday."

"She must have forgotten." She did a quick calculation for how many days left of the ten days that a mother had of rest after giving birth. "It's now four days?"

Rhea smiled and nodded. "Yes, four."

"I see. Then I'll visit tomorrow."

"I'm sure Gerda would like that. I recall my ten days with Rahel. It became monotonous after a while. I now think how foolish I was. I should have simply enjoyed that time."

Dora smiled. "I'll go fetch Anya."

She entered the house and saw her niece eating the cold remains of beans. "Rhea is outside waiting for you. It's fortunate that you have something in your stomach."

Anya swallowed and put down her spoon. "She's waiting for me?" She seemed chagrined. "I forgot. I'm sorry."

"Hmmph. Never mind that. Go tend to Gerda." Anya seemed to want to say something. "Do well. When you come home, you can help with the chores and with a salve. There's one plant that we need and I'll show you where it grows and what it looks like. Then we can work on your new skirt together. Si?"

"Si, Tia."

"Good. With a little work, your other skirt will be fine for Roza."

Danel joined Dora and watched their niece leave. He murmured, "Where did she learn such stubbornness? So headstrong."

"I can only imagine." Dora looked at him, wondering if he was being serious or sarcastic.

"I have an idea that we must discuss when we're alone," he replied.

* * *

"Anya, look in the basket," Danel said from the front of the wagon. "It's time to eat." Danel's idea had been to take Anya to Grantville, and they were now at the very outskirts of the town.

From her place in the back of the crate-filled wagon, she removed the cloth covering the food and handed her tio and Jörg Ruprecht, the foreman, a pastry filled with vegetables. Dora had made them the previous day, so there would be no need to patronize a tavern or public house when they entered Grantville. *"All we need is for our Anya to be adversely influenced by such people."*

Anya took the third pastry and bit into it. She had never eaten anything like it before. One of the ladies from the synagogue told Tia how to make them. After a few bites, she took out the jug of small beer.

Danel reached back and she placed the jug in his waiting hand.

"Your wife's a good cook."

"Thank you. A drink?" The jug was passed between the two men.

Anya's eyes widened at the sight of large, brightly colored houses set back from the road and then a cluster of big, official-looking buildings off to the right. She turned away so that she wouldn't see the immodesty. Papa was right! There were women who dressed like sailors! She couldn't help but twist around behind when she was startled by an unusual, loud rumbling. She gawked, gape-mouthed at the strange carriage following them without a horse. She took in all the people and sights all at once. She had never seen so many different people all bustling about their day. Even the many buildings looked out of place. She rubbed her nose to stop it from tingling from all the strange scents.

"Jörg. That building there." Danel pointed. "Anya and I will discuss matters with..." His brows creased and then his face relaxed when he remembered the term. "...the *nursing director*. You are to come to us after you finish delivering juice and oranges."

"I'll be quick about it."

Danel and she watched the foreman maneuver the wagon back onto the main street once they were in front of the building. "The only one in my employ that can be trusted with money," Danel said to himself. Then, to Anya, "Come along."

Anya followed him into the building. She looked around, wanting to touch the walls and the flooring, but she didn't want to appear foolish. What paint did they use for the walls? What were the floors made of?

Then there were the people. A few women walked past, wearing plain dresses with either a short simple apron or a long apron with frills and soft-soled shoes favored by some Spaniards. They also wore similarly shaped pins. She made note that she would need to keep her hair as neat and tidy as the women she observed. She smiled, knowing that she would be joining them soon enough. One woman who wore a strange cap and a long apron with frills gave instructions to a younger woman wearing a shorter apron with no frills. The young woman gave a quick acknowledgment before scurrying away. Anya understood the woman with the frilled apron was the younger woman's better.

They approached a desk where people seemed to be asking questions. "Good day," Danel said, giving a small neck bow. "I'm Herr Nahon and this is my niece, Anya." Anya curtsied.

"Good day. No need for bowing or curtseying here in Grantville. What can I help you find?" They were clearly not the first newcomers the receptionist had met.

"Would you please tell us how to find Herr Director Garnet Szymanski?"

Quickly assessing Anya and her uncle, she said, "Yes, follow me."

They entered an office, and a woman sitting behind a desk stopped writing as the three approached.

"Greta, this is Herr..."

"Danel Nahon," he offered with a shallow bow.

"Nahon. And his niece." Anya curtsied. "They're here to see the director."

"Of course. You have an appointment. I'll be right back."

"I'll leave you now," said Susanne.

Greta quickly came out of the office. "Please come in."

A woman greeted them. "Good day, I'm Garnet Szymanski, the director. Thank you for coming."

Anya was surprised: A woman is in charge?! Her uncle seemed just as amazed, but quickly recovered. He bowed. "It was very generous of you to agree to see us."

"Not at all. Please,"—she directed them to the two empty chairs in front of her desk—"take a seat, and we'll discuss Anya's possible admission to our program."

"Thank you," Danel said.

"Tell me, Anya, why do you want to be a nurse?"

Anya swallowed, looking at her tio for his assistance. He looked at her, encouraging her to speak. Addressing the director, she said timidly in her best German, "I want to take care of the sick."

"I see. Is there another reason?"

"She's becoming an accomplished midwife. Yet, she has told my wife and me several times that her desire, above all else, is to become a nurse."

The director looked at Danel and then back to Anya. Anya looked so relieved that he had spoken for her.

"Anya, I would rather you answer for yourself. I know some down-timers think of people like me as *adel* and it can be scary to talk to us, but you don't need to be afraid. Okay?" She waited for Anya's nod. "Good. A midwife? How wonderful. Then you may want to be certified as a midwife with us—Level One. Level Two would require knowledge of some up-time technique. We instruct our nurses in how to heal the wounded in battle as well as those who are ill or dying. Some of our nurses also travel during the winter."

If she were married as Tio, Tia, and Papa wanted, would her husband allow her to heal the battle wounded or travel?

"Nursing requires a lot of studying and reading. Do you know how to read German?"

Anya cast her eyes down in embarrassment. She could barely read and write in her native language. Tio appeared to be sympathetic when she looked to him for help.

"She is learning to speak German well," he said, still looking at her.

The director nodded. "You need to read and speak English as well as German, Anya. If you're willing, we can make sure that you're able to read and write in English and German while you also learn the skills necessary for our program. Are you willing to do all this extra work?"

Anya thought for only a moment, excited by the opportunity. Of course, she would work very hard! There was no question that she wouldn't.

Danel looked at Anya's elated face. "My wife and I will need to discuss such a generous offer."

"Yes," Garnet answered him. Then, to Anya, "I hope you return to us—"

Anya didn't listen to anything else after that. She was upset and felt betrayed. Wasn't coming here her uncle's idea? Could he be as cruel as her father? Making promises that vanished like morning dew? Numbly, she followed her tio out of the office.

Danel looked at the dish on the reception desk as they passed.

"Please, help yourselves to a mint candy," the receptionist offered.

"Thank you," Danel picked one up and proffered it to Anya. She shook her head and he took the treat instead. "Hmm."

Her head held down, she followed her uncle outside. She refused to make eye contact with him.

"We have time. I know of a wonderful confectionary. Whenever I need to be here in Grantville, I indulge in the shop's sweets. And I think something may help. Come." He gave her a mischievous smile. "Don't tell your tia. It'll be our secret."

"Si, Tio." She followed him down the long street. Grantville no longer held the sparkle it had for her when they first arrived. Even the candy he purchased for them wasn't as enjoyable as it should have been.

They were heading back when Tio stopped and stepped over to the side so that other pedestrians could pass them. "Anya, I brought you here for a purpose —"

She blurted out, "It was cruel."

He took a breath and finished. "Your abuelo, our father, favored your papa because he was the first son. I truly believed this." She looked squarely at him at the mention of Papa. "I was barely twelve and wanted to join my other two friends to go on a trading ship. Abuelo had secured a fine apprenticeship for your papa and thought that he would do the same for me."

"What happened?"

"He refused to let me go. I sneaked to the port to join my friends. I was told that only two of us were needed; I wasn't chosen." He pursed his lips in thought. "I bid farewell to my friends." He popped another piece of candy in his mouth and chewed. "I returned home. Papa found an apprenticeship for me, and I hated him for it. I wanted to be a sailor. After a year's time, I went down to the docks for my friends' return and learned that they had died. One of illness, the other...the other from wounds received in an unsavory fight."

"But, Tio, I don't want to be a sailor."

"Yes, yes. We worry for you, your tia and I. We want to protect you. I was worried that you would come here anyway. You are strong-willed, even for a young woman. I don't know if it's in your blood as a Nahon or up-time influences."

He was right, she would have. "Tio, I want to learn how to read."

"We will discuss this further. Now then, let us return to the hospital. Hopefully, Jörg is waiting for us."

Anya thought about what Tio said during the journey home. She wouldn't allow herself to think about Tio's story any more. She was going to train in Grantville to become a nurse. She just knew that Tio and Tia would help her—and Papa too.

The Redbird Reader
(fiction)

Flint's Shards, Inc.

The Guardians Of Germany

Bjorn Hasseler

This story pulls together Wilhelm Reuber ("The Slasher," Grantville Gazette 61), Christoph von Hessler ("The Saale Levies," Grantville Gazette 56), and Sunshine Moritz (Security Solutions).

Jena

July 1636

Johann Markus Schrön warily pushed open the door of the inn in Jena. It seemed clean enough. In fact, it was so clean that he immediately suspected the innkeeper of being an adherent of the Committees of Correspondence. They weren't his favorite people, but it did mean he could trust the food and drink. That was good to know.

"Over here, Johann Markus!" Kaspar Both called.

Johann Markus had no trouble spotting Kaspar and his friend Wilhelm Reuber at the far end of the room. The lighting was good, too. He made his way over and sat down.

A server materialized at his side. "We have mutton or Amideutsch stew."

"Amideutsch stew has both beef and mutton," Wilhelm put in.

"Mutton stew," Johann Markus answered.

"Bread or fries?"

He made a face. "The bread."

"Small beer or root beer?"

"Definitely small beer."

Once the server left with his order, Johann Markus asked, "Why are we meeting here?"

"So we will not be overheard," Kaspar told him. "The owner is CoC, as are any students likely to come in."

Johann Markus nodded at that confirmation.

Reuber and Both exchanged glances, then Kaspar Both said, "We both come from prosperous families. Our fathers are both masters of their crafts and influential in their towns. From what you've said, your father seems to be in a similar position."

"He is a member of the *rat*." Johann Markus' voice was stiff.

Kaspar just nodded and gestured toward Wilhelm. "We have both found that there is prosperous, and then there is *prosperous*. To be blunt, our funds are very limited from time to time."

Johann Markus rolled his eyes. "And now you will tell me how you can afford to attend the university. Is it unethical or merely disreputable?"

Wilhelm laughed. "See, I told you, Kaspar! He is quick."

Kaspar Both nodded in acknowledgement.

"We turned to writing," Wilhelm went on.

"Writing?" Johann Markus asked.

Wilhelm reached for something on the bench beside him and laid a book on the table.

"*The Mystery of the Crusader's Sword*," Johann Markus read. "But the author is Franklin W. Dixon. An up-timer, clearly."

"This is part of the Hardy Boys series," Wilhelm explained. "All the authors use the *nom de plume* Franklin W. Dixon. But I assure you, this one was written by Wilhelm Reuber." He laid another book on the table.

"*The Mystery of the Train Robbery*," Johann Markus read. "I take it Carolyn Keene is another *nom de plume*?"

"*Ja*. These are up-time detective stories."

Johann Markus nodded. Every University of Jena student knew about detectives. Even one of Jena's own judges, Pieter Freihofer, had adopted their methods last year.

Reuber added a third book.

"*The Guardians of Germany*." Johann Markus considered it. "This is not a detective story."

"No, it is closest to what the up-timers call a superhero series."

Johann Markus hadn't fallen off the turnip cart just yesterday. "Myths, in other words."

"Ja."

"The series is the mythic cycle," Johann Markus surmised. "Ancient myths were at odds with each other. Different versions of the same story, sometimes with different figures involved. Are the up-timers' superhero series like that?"

"*Ja*, they are," Reuber told him.

Johann Markus pointed to the *Guardians of Germany* volume. "And these?"

"No, we maintain continuity," Kaspar answered. "Wilhelm is quite fanatical about it."

Reuber made a shooing motion. "It is poor craftsmanship to contradict yourself."

Johann Markus smiled. "So you are doing it right. And I take it you want me to help."

"Your rhetoric is quite good, and you write well. If, from time to time, you find yourself in similar circumstances to us..."

"Why share?" Johann Markus' tone was blunt.

"Because we cannot keep up," Kaspar stated. "Wilhelm has written five books in the past two years. As much as it pains me to admit it, he is the most productive of us."

"And you?"

"I have written three."

"How many more of you are there?"

"Good question," Kaspar told Johann Markus. "There are five of us."

"Six," Wilhelm countered.

"Six, if you count Hans who wrote one book and has been saying for a year that he will write another one soon."

Johann Markus sat back and crossed his arms. "How many books can people read? Does anyone buy them?"

"I told you he would ask," Kaspar reminded Wilhelm.

"You did," Wilhelm acknowledged. He turned back to Johann Markus. "They sell in Grantville, Magdeburg, the Leipzig book fair, the Wish Book. My *Guardians of Germany: The Saxon Ghost* may sell a few hundred copies."

"What do you get per copy?"

"A couple bucks."

Johann Markus drew a deep breath. "All right. Tell me how the *Guardians of Germany* works. What's the mythology?"

Wilhelm and Kaspar exchanged triumphant smiles.

"Frederick Barbarossa is king under the mountain," Kaspar began.

"Kyffhauser," Johann Markus put in.

"He's awake. After seeing the devastation of the wars, he appealed for protection for the Germanies. He's able to nudge things along by subtly helping chosen heroes."

"This sounds pretty pagan. What is the Church going to say?"

"Barbarossa appealed to God," Wilhelm clarified.

"What about these heroes? Who are they?"

"Each hero gets his own book. So far, I have written *The Saxon Ghost* and *The Slasher*. Next I am writing *The Baroness*—and I am searching for what comes after that."

"Julie Sims?"

"*Nein*, she will be based on Christina von Burkersroda." Wilhelm gave Johann Markus a quick summary.

"So no up-timers?" Johann Markus sought clarification.

"Yes and no. We write as though the Prince of Germany and *Der Adler* and Julie Sims are among the heroes, but we say there is no need for those books because everyone knows the stories already."

"What else?"

"I think we should drop hints that Barbarossa isn't the only king under the mountain," Wilhelm suggested. "Bohemia has Wenceslaus, England has Arthur..."

"This is the part that sounds very pagan," Johann Markus pointed out.

"He is correct," Kaspar agreed. "Wilhelm, Dr. Himmel is already giving you dark looks."

"...and Israel has David," Reuber finished. "Says so in one of the prophets, long after David died."

"I think that's talking about the new heavens and the new earth."

Reuber threw up his arms. "Have you heard the theology professors arguing about the end times? There are as many new theories as there are up-timers. Nobody agrees. Compared to that, nobody will care about kings under mountains."

"Do all countries get them? What about, say, France?"

Wilhelm drummed his fingers on the table and thought. "Richelieu *is* missing, you know. Maybe dead, maybe not."

"You'd give the French *Richelieu*?" Johann Markus demanded.

"Sure, why not? He can be at odds with Barbarossa. We need a bad guy."

Johann Markus rolled his eyes. "And the up-timers? Do they have one?"

"They didn't have kings. 'President under the mountain' sounds silly. And their Washington didn't disappear, so we can't really use him."

"Did any famous Americans disappear in the up-time?"

"I don't know. We could have a library researcher find out." Wilhelm thought about it. "We'd have to send someone to Grantville to hire the researcher. This isn't the sort of request that would make sense by telephone or telegraph."

"That is fine," Kaspar told him. "I have been wanting to visit Grantville again anyway. Let us spend a few days. Their summer *messe* and Fourth of July have passed, but there is a lot of summer left."

Reuber considered that. "As long as we ride," he said. "I can't afford to take the train *just because*, as the up-timers say. Only when it is truly necessary." He currently defined necessary as travel between Magdeburg and the University of Jena. He didn't stop to think that as little as three years ago, he had ridden a horse that whole way and thought nothing of it.

State Library, Grantville

A couple weeks later, Wilhelm Reuber, Kaspar Both, and Johann Markus Schrön made their way to Grantville High School. Finding the State Library was not hard; getting in was. There was a long line at the counter, and it moved slowly.

"We would like to hire a researcher," Kaspar told the woman behind the counter when they finally reached the front of the line.

"I will see who is free." She ran her finger down a page in front of her before looking back up at them. "Mathew Woodruff is taking new clients."

The three of them exchanged glances. Wilhelm shrugged. "Why not?"

"Where may we meet *Herr* Woodruff?" Kaspar asked.

* * *

Woodruff turned out to be an Englishman, tall for a down-timer.

"With what may I help you?" he asked.

"Can you keep a secret?" Kaspar asked.

"When one of us researches a topic, he makes a copy of the report for the client, and a second copy is put on file," Woodruff explained. "Then the next time someone wants information on that topic, he can buy the report or request further research. But that is a gamble. Sometimes no new information is found, but the research time costs money, whether it is successful or not."

"So someone else could buy the same information and publish first," Johann Markus observed.

"The State Library does not allow a monopoly on any knowledge. If it is here on these shelves, anyone may research it." His bland manner told Wilhelm that he had explained this many times.

Wilhelm traded looks with Kaspar and Johann Markus again. At their nods, he told Woodruff, "We are looking for missing up-timers."

Woodruff frowned. "I do not believe any up-timers are missing."

"*Nein, nein.* Up-timers who went missing in the up-time. Or have a legend that they will come back." Wilhelm explained what they had in mind.

"I am not sure that anyone has asked this before," Woodruff told them. "I will look into it. Let us discuss rates..."

Camp Saale
July 1636

"All right. Let's break for lunch," Major Blodger suggested.

Christoph shook his head. He could do that now without his head swimming. The latest of a succession of fevers had broken some weeks before, and Colonel von Sparr had decided a change of surroundings would do him good. As soon as Christoph could stay on a horse all day, his commanding officer had sent him as part of a group of couriers to the other Colonel von Sparr, to work out a way for the regiment to ride to the defense of Vienna.

He hadn't grasped just how much the world had changed.

A patrol sent out by General Brahe had intercepted them almost as soon as they'd entered the USE. Brahe had heard them out. Then they'd been very efficiently handed off from one unit to another, until they arrived at Erfurt. There they'd been bundled onto a train and sent to Camp Saale by way of Jena. He hadn't even had time to go home. Home was nearby, in a tongue of electoral Saxony that projected out into the jumble of smaller states that was apparently now the State of Thuringia-Franconia. He wondered how his brothers Georg Rudolph, Hans Heinrich, and Hans Friedrich were. His sisters were all married and, last he knew, living not too far away.

Christoph knew he was gawking, and he hadn't even seen Grantville itself yet. Camp Saale was both a State of Thuringia-Franconia National Guard encampment and a major supply depot for the USE Army. Supplies moved in and out all the time, supply trains ran south, and most impressive of all, everyone seemed to know what he was doing.

Or what *she* was doing. He'd seen a few women in USE gray and more in SoTF blue. But then halfway through a discussion of what the up-timers called tactical railroad, someone had clarified that Colonel Pitre's first name was Elizabeth.

His head was spinning. But at least it wasn't from sickness this time.

"This is the mess hall," his guide said.

It looked like an oversized tavern. Christoph and his fellow couriers joined a line of men. Each was handed a tray of food. They collected small beer and found places at a table.

"What is this?" Christoph asked. "Horse?"

"*Nein.* Do not even joke about that."

Christoph frowned. "Why not? What is it, then?"

"Beef."

"To impress us?"

"*Nein.* Because up-timers eat a lot of beef. Remember the Israelites in the wilderness eating quail and manna until they were sick of it? That is up-timers, cooking beef for the rest of us." The guide gave a wry grin. "You may have noticed, though, they tend to be bigger."

As a matter of fact, he had.

The food was strange, but filling. Once they were done eating, their guide stood.

Redbird Institute

Sunshine Moritz stood there in a flannel shirt, jeans, boots, and a hard hat, impatiently tapping her toe.

This particular construction crew was finally ready to raise the side of a new retreat center on the east side of the lake. Foreman Hale Pomeroy was off with her dad, walking the ground for an upcoming project, so Sunshine was subbing for him. The Happy Acres team was a well-oiled machine, Redbird's Brethren had a vested interest in finishing the project, and the rest of Redbird's "brown sleeves" were solid. The three could join forces to put up a fancy chalet in just a couple weeks, but they just hadn't meshed on this project.

"Use. The. Come-along." Sunshine didn't quite growl the words. "It is safe. It is even less work."

"We have always done it this way," one of the men protested.

"Change."

Camp Saale

After lunch, they hit a snag. All the National Guard brass who could give permission for von Sparr's regiment to cross the State of Thuringia-Franconia on its way to Vienna were in a meeting...probably about Vienna.

"Well," Major Blodger said, "there's nothing we can do about it. Lieutenant Topf, why don't you give our guests the grand tour?"

Topf looked dubious. "A Grantville tour usually takes all day, sir. There's some relevant training going on at the lake, though. It's different units, retainers mostly, learning to work together. I could see if there's a pickup available and take them out there."

"It's a nice place," the major agreed. "Okay, save Grantville for tomorrow or the next day so they get the full effect."

* * *

In less time than Christoph von Hessler imagined, he, his fellow couriers, and the lieutenant were in the back of a *pickup truck*, rumbling toward...he didn't know what. What he'd heard was a stream of conflicting ideas, including "garden palace," "salon," "playground for the *adel*," and "training ground."

The vehicle they rode in followed a dirt road, graveled in places, out into the countryside.

"This is faster than a horse!" one of the other couriers exclaimed.

The lieutenant slid part of the cab's rear window open and spoke to the sergeant who was driving.

"We are going fifteen miles per hour. If this were the sort of road you will see in Grantville, we could go much faster."

Christoph shook his head. He'd heard about the up-time vehicles—who hadn't?—but the way they casually used this one for what was essentially an afternoon's entertainment spoke volumes.

"Hang on tight," Topf directed.

The truck started up a steep hill. Christoph felt a bit of a twinge. He hoped it was because they were driving up what seemed like a cliff rather than because the fevers were returning. When the vehicle crested the hill, they glimpsed a lake nestled between the hills. Tasteful cottages were scattered about, with what looked like a large *schloss* overlooking the lake. A few other buildings were grouped near it, and all of them blended into their setting even though their construction seemed outlandish at the same time.

The sergeant driving the pickup selected a pathway that was little more than a dirt trail, but it led around the lake. Christoph had to admit it was a scenic place. On the far side, workmen were raising some new structure. A wall went up even as they passed by.

The truck coasted to a stop. The lieutenant hopped over the side, then lowered the tailgate for the others. They piled out and admired the lake.

Christoph von Hessler followed the others. Lunch wasn't settling well, and the ride in the back of the pickup truck had left him decidedly queasy. A horse he could have handled, although being honest with himself, he would have avoided a trot right now.

Hopefully this tour wouldn't take too long, and he could discreetly retire to whatever quarters the SoTF National Guard had arranged.

One of his fellow couriers pointed at a boat out on the lake. He said something about the rigging, but it meant nothing to Christoph. The only boat he'd ever been on was a raft that crossed the Saale River at Naumburg.

Christoph stepped up on some rocks to maximize a welcome breeze. From there, he could look almost straight down at the lake. From the conversation behind him, he gathered the remarkable thing about the boat was how close to the wind it sailed.

Then another wave of queasiness struck, and Christoph concentrated on not throwing up. The wind gusted. The horizon dipped slightly, balanced out, and dipped again. Then all Christoph von Hessler felt was the rushing wind—until he struck the water, hard.

* * *

"Hilfe! Hilfe!"

Sunshine Moritz heard the call for help and jerked around. She saw the parked pickup and the men who'd been riding in it clustered at the edge of the bluff. Someone pointed, and she knew.

Sunshine undid her cuff buttons and took off running. It wasn't her absolute fastest, because she was hyperventilating and unbuttoning her work shirt as she ran. She ditched the shirt along the way.

"Did someone fall in?"

"Ja." One of the men turned to face her. "Von Hessler—You aren't even looking at me!"

Sunshine dropped one boot, undid the laces on the other, and pulled it off.

"Right off these rocks?"

She shrugged out of her jeans while asking the question and then tossed her hard hat.

"*Ja*, but—"

"Someone, take the truck to the lodge and get a lifeguard!"

Sunshine took three running steps across the rocks and jumped.

* * *

Wilhelm Reuber, Kaspar Both, and Johann Markus Schrön were at loose ends. Woodruff was researching for them. They'd been interviewing up-timers, first on the street and then by the simple expedient of finding taverns and buying them beers.

"We could keep this up until we are drunk," Johann Markus stated.

"Hear, hear!" Kaspar said.

"But we are getting nowhere," Johann Markus finished.

"That is not true," Wilhelm insisted. "Not entirely. We have names of several up-timers who disappeared." He read the list. "Jimmy Hoffa, Judge Crater..."

"There are three, not several," Johann Markus pointed out. "*Und* Jimmy Hoffa is not suitable. He is a criminal."

Wilhelm reluctantly crossed out the name.

"*Und* no one seems to remember much about this judge."

"What about the woman?" Johann Markus asked. "Amelia Earhart? How will that be received?"

Wilhelm shrugged. "I do not foresee any problem...except that so many up-timers mentioned her that perhaps it is too easy a solution."

"It is time to try a different approach," Kaspar stated. "We have a researcher. We have asked up-timers, but these are working men. We need to ask the sort of person who knows their tales and literature and history."

"A teacher?" Johann Markus suggested.

"*Nein*. Finish your beers. We need to find one of their salons, where people trade in knowledge."

* * *

"A salon? Well, if you want high falutin', it's out at that Redbird place."

"Redbird?"

"Nerd Disney. It's out in the eastern lobe of the county, up north of Saalfeld. I think I heard there's some new sort of train."

* * *

Wilhelm Reuber read the bulletin board posted outside the Redbird Institute's grand lodge. "Sailing demonstrations all day. A lecture on art this afternoon. Flight tomorrow. Astronomy tomorrow night. We must make a habit of this."

"Are you sure it wasn't the pretty *fräuleins* we saw?" Kaspar Both asked.

"Sailing demonstration. What do you suppose that is?" Wilhelm wondered.

"Well, it must be on the lake. We can probably see it from the shore. Come on." Wilhelm set out toward the lake. It was some distance away from the grand lodge and downhill. Apparently, the lake was expected to rise.

It took just a few minutes to reach the water's edge, and a sailboat was clearly visible.

"I think the demonstration is over," Johann Markus said. "It appears to be coming back toward the dock."

"What do you suppose it is demonstrating?" Wilhelm asked. "We might be able to see the last bit."

"I have no idea," Kaspar replied. "I have never been on a boat. It could do some up-time thing, and I would not know the difference."

"Nor I," Wilhelm agreed.

"Let us walk over and ask," Johann Markus suggested.

As the boat coasted toward one of the docks, the crew struck the sail. Two men on the docks reached out long poles with hooks on the end, snared the boat, and pulled it alongside the dock. A crewman tossed ropes, and the two men on shore tied up the craft. Then the men on the dock helped three passengers disembark.

Two of the passengers wore fine fabrics while the other wore plainer clothes. Wilhelm wondered about that for a moment but was distracted by a shouted question from the boat.

"Are you the next group?"

"What?"

"Are you the next group?"

This time Wilhelm identified the speaker as an older, bearded man wearing an elaborate cap.

"Oh, *nein*!" he shouted back.

"I do not see anyone else here. Do you want to sail into the wind?"

The university students exchanged glances.

"Sure! *Danke!*"

The three scrambled aboard.

"May I have your attention, *bitte*? *Ich heisse* Heinrich Siemssen. I am the captain of this vessel. The *Neuheit* is fore-and-aft rigged. The up-time rigging allows her to sail very close to the wind. But sometimes we have to adjust the sails, and if I ask you to get down on the deck, it is for your own safety—so the boom does not hit you. Do you all understand? I do not want you to get hit and swept overboard."

A chorus of *jas* answered him. Captain Siemssen and his single crewman got to work, and soon the *Neuheit* was underway. Sooner than Wilhelm expected, they were skimming across the lake.

Siemssen gave orders, and soon he and the crewman demonstrated what the new rigging let them do. Wilhelm heard most of it but understood only generalities.

"Look, there are people watching atop that cliff." Kaspar pointed off to the left at the far shore of the narrow lake

"Where?" Wilhelm followed Kaspar's pointing finger. "Oh, I see them."

Then to his horror, one of them pitched off the cliff.

"*Nein!*" Wilhelm cried. "Captain!"

"I saw! Bring us about!" Siemssen added several orders, none of which meant anything to Wilhelm.

"Look!" Johann Markus cried.

A slender figure was running along the spit of land, shedding clothes. Then the figure jumped from the cliff.

"Who is he?" Wilhelm wondered.

"She," Johann Markus corrected.

"Down!" Captain Siemssen ordered.

They dropped to the deck and lost sight of the figure.

* * *

Sunshine felt the shock as she hit the water. It wasn't the twenty-foot drop. It was the temperature. The lake was *cold*.

She'd scissors-kicked as she hit to slow her drop. Sunshine figured she went about eight feet below the surface. She'd hyperventilated, so she had oxygen. There was no reason to surface until she had to.

What she needed to know was how deep the lake was right here. She struck out toward where she thought the man had gone down. Once she was away from her own splash, she could see the bottom dimly. It looked about four feet away. She continued in that direction.

Nothing. Sunshine kicked for the surface.

She gulped oxygen, then looked to the cliff face. There were concerned faces up there.

"One of you stand where he was!" she called.

One of the faces moved sideways. Sunshine saw she was still short of the spot.

"*Dank!*" She swam that way and dove.

This lake was a lot like the Ring lakes. The new dam had flooded a valley, so the bottom was grass or dirt. *Dead* grass. Sunshine knew they'd logged every tree first. Because wood was always in demand—and because a dead, drowned tree growing up out of a lake would be just plain freaky.

There!

He'd drifted a bit as he sank, so there must be a weak current along the cliff face, pulling out toward...well, toward the dam, obviously.

She reached the man, turned him over, put an arm across his chest, and pushed off the bottom for all she was worth.

Sunshine swam for the surface. She almost didn't make it. After the ten feet that would have gotten her from the bottom of the Grantville municipal pool to the open air, she was still underwater. She scissors-kicked and swam with one arm.

Her head broke the surface, and she gulped air. The man almost slipped from her grasp. She pulled him up, got his face out of the water.

Not breathing. Can't find a pulse, but that could just be me. Can't fix that in the water anyway.

Sunshine gave him mouth-to-mouth. He coughed up water. At her. Sunshine said a word her parents didn't approve of and did what she could to pound the man on the back.

"Are you okay? Are you okay? Can you hear me?"

"So cold," the man murmured. Then he coughed again.

This time Sunshine had him aimed away from her.

"Do you know how to float? Lie back, and I'll tow you to shore."

Whatever the man did, he dropped like a stone. Sunshine gulped a quick breath and went after him. She grabbed him about two feet down and got them back to the surface.

Boots, she realized.

There was no way she could get his boots off, and she didn't think he was up to doing it himself. *No choice. This is going to suck.* She could, however, get rid of his coat and quickly undid the buttons. Then it took a couple minutes to get his arms out of the sleeves,

Sunshine lay back in the water, keeping her left arm across his chest. She set out in an awkward sidestroke. From the looks of the cliff, she was going to have to swim him all the way back to where her crew was putting in the new building.

Sweep. Kick. Sweep. Kick. *He's going to be hypothermic before we get there.*

Then Sunshine heard shouting. She glanced up at the cliff and saw the faces there were moving along with her and the man. And they were pointing. At something beyond her, she thought.

The sidestroke had her back to whatever it was. Sunshine stopped and treaded water for a moment so she could turn.

A boat! *Awesome!*

A fast one, too. She saw a bit of white water at the bow.

Sunshine resumed her sidestroke, pulling the man toward where she figured the boat would be. A couple minutes later, she could hear shouted commands. Presumably that was sailboat-speak for "Stop!"

They tossed her a rope.

"Gee, thanks," Sunshine muttered. *What I want is one of those rope mesh net thingies.* But she managed to wrap it under the man's arms and tie it with the world's most unnautical knot, complete with a big bow.

"Okay! Pull!"

The crew hoisted the man aboard.

Sunshine didn't wait for the rope to return. Up-time boats often had a step in the stern... *Yes!* She scrambled up, and a couple of people stepped forward to help her over the railing.

"Thanks."

"My pleasure."

One corner of Sunshine's mind cataloged *three guys, kinda cute,* as she made a beeline for the man who'd fallen into the lake.

"Please! Let me through!"

The two crewmen looked at her with startled expressions but got out of the way.

Sunshine knelt beside him and quickly undid the knot. She put her ear near his mouth. "Breathing." Felt for a pulse. "Pulse." She counted. "Not a good one. Can you hear me? Can you hear me?"

The man moaned.

"You fell in. Are you okay? Does anything hurt?" *He probably doesn't speak English, dummy.* Sunshine repeated herself in German.

"*Kalt,*" the man mumbled.

Sunshine looked up. "Do you have blankets?"

Someone found something that wasn't quite a blanket, but it would do. Sunshine tucked it around him. She looked up again. "Can we get him to shore as quickly as possible? I think he needs a hospital."

* * *

Wilhelm knew he was staring at the girl. She wore what he could only assume was underwear and a top that other than covering her breasts seemed to be made mostly of string. She was dripping wet, of course.

She looked up just then, eyes searching the people crowded around until they picked out Siemssen.

"Captain? I apologize for commandeering your boat...ship...whatever. We need to get this man to a hospital."

"I have a radio, and this schooner rig lets us sail close to the wind," Siemssen told her.

"Please call shore and have them call the rescue squad in Grantville. I need Hawker Baldwin if he's available. Do you know the staff here? Lifeguard Elias Ramsenthaler?"

"*Ja*, I know the name. He teaches people to swim."

Sunshine smiled briefly. "Right. If he could meet us at the dock?"

Captain Siemssen spoke into the radio. "Redbird, *Neuheit*. Call the rescue squad and Hawker Baldwin. Send lifeguard Elias Ramsenthaler to the dock."

Then he gave orders. Sunshine didn't understand anything beyond "into the wind."

"Not exactly a down-time Scarab, is it?" Sunshine muttered. "Or, maybe, it is."

Wilhelm finally glanced at his comrades. Kaspar was just as focused on the girl as he'd been. But Johann Markus...Johann Markus was entranced.

Wilhelm poked him a couple times.

"What?"

Wilhelm spoke quietly. "*Ja*, she is pretty. *Ja*, she is not wearing much. *Ja*, she is wet."

"I know all that." Johann Markus finally looked away, directly at Wilhelm and Kaspar. "I know what book to write. *The Naiad*."

Kaspar laughed.

Wilhelm groaned. "Johann Markus, you have it bad—"

"Have either of you explained for the series how Friedrich Barbarossa did not really drown?" Johann Markus interrupted.

"*Nein*, b—"

"I know how—the naiad."

"That is..." Wilhelm began.

"Brilliant," Kaspar stated. "Write it. But *naiad* is Greek. Call it *Die Nixe*, or even *The Mermaid*."

* * *

Sunshine knelt next to the man, monitoring his vital signs. He was breathing and had a pulse. But unless she was misreading the signs, he was at least in shock and probably had hypothermia. She ran her hands down his arms and legs, checking for broken bones, but found none.

"Can you hear me?" she asked.

"*Ja*." The answer was weaker than Sunshine was comfortable with.

"Does your head ache?"

He mumbled something she couldn't understand. She repeated the question.

"Nein."

"How is your vision?"

"*Gut*, I think."

"Are you dizzy? Do you have a metallic taste in your mouth?"

"Nein."

"Probably not a concussion," Sunshine murmured.

"Cold. Dizzy."

"Maybe a concussion," she amended. "How did you fall?"

"Dizzy."

"You were dizzy before you fell in?"

"*Ja*. Was sick. Thought I was better."

Oh, great, Sunshine thought. I hope I didn't catch whatever it is.

The boat reached the dock in minutes. "Much faster than any other rig could have done," Captain Siemssen boasted.

"Thanks," Sunshine told him. She spotted a young man her age running toward the dock. "Elias!"

He ran up as Sunshine was directing the others.

"Let's get him off the boat and inside. Which building is the warmest?" She saw mostly blank looks.

Elias pointed. "That one. It has a room with south-facing windows."

"Let's get him over there."

Sunshine eased the man's shoulders up and slid both arms behind them. She nodded at Johann Markus. "Cross your wrists and take my hands." Then at Wilhelm and Caspar. "Do the same for his legs."

"Now lift." They picked the man up.

"Pass him over," Elias directed. He and one of the dockhands supported the man's shoulders as Sunshine and Johann Markus dropped away. Sunshine put one hand on the boat's gunwale and swung herself down to the dock. Then she and the other dockhand linked hands to support the man's legs.

They got the man up a hill to a beautiful asymmetrical half-timber building. From previous visits, she knew its four lobes were each suitable for a lecture, chamber concert, art exhibition, or salon. A central node held a warming kitchen and the restrooms.

Wilhelm Reuber sped past them to doors that opened out onto a flagstone patio. He and Captain Siemssen held the double doors open as the others carried the man inside.

Sunshine took a quick look around. The room wasn't yet set up and held no chairs or tables.

"The floor it is. Down on three."

Once the man was on the floor, Sunshine tucked the blanket or whatever it was around him.

"What is this thing, anyway?"

Wilhelm supplied the word. "A tarpaulin. Found in up-time boats."

"Why do you know that?"

"The Hardy Boys."

Sunshine just shook her head.

It wasn't long before they heard an ambulance siren. It pulled up outside the building, and another vehicle skidded to a stop behind it.

Hawker Baldwin was the first through the door. "What happened, Sunshine?"

"He fell off the rocks on the east shore. We're building a retreat center and a new campground over there, so I wasn't too far away." She waved a hand. "Captain Siemssen was out on the lake, picked us up, and got us over here."

One of the rescue squad paramedics looked up from examining the man. "Lucky they were there. He's...I dunno. It presents like hypothermia, but I don't think it is."

"Take us through the rescue, Sunshine," Hawker directed.

Sunshine did so.

"Good job. You need to get checked out."

"For what?"

"If it's not hypothermia, it could be a fever, malaria, any number of things. You were rescue breathing."

Sunshine sobered. "I know—and that's a little scary. But my work clothes and boots are on the other side of the lake."

Hawker cocked his head. "You weren't by chance thinking of swimming back over there to pick them up, were you?"

Sunshine didn't quite look him in the face. "My crew and my ride are both over there. Besides, I don't think anyone has swum across the lake yet..."

"Sunshine!"

"Wanna come along?"

Hawker gave her a deflating look. "I'll drive you around the lake to get your stuff if you promise to drop by Leahy tomorrow. Or sooner, if you feel sick."

"Hawker..."

"And I'll swim the lake with you as long as there's a boat tracking us."

She nodded slowly. "When?"

"Sunday?"

"I guess it'll have to be Sunday afternoon." Sunshine shrugged. "I kinda told the girls I'd go to church with them. Much as I'd rather sleep through it."

Hawker's face held a curious expression. "Does this have anything to do with—?"

"Friedrich?" Sunshine shook her head. "Nope. His sister is making him go to St. Martin's in the Fields. No, it's Barbara, Regina, Astrid, and Eva Želivský."

* * *

The king sat unmoving, staring at the map of Europe spread across the old wooden table. His hair was long and unkempt as though he had been there long years. A dim light suffused the stone chamber.

Something hammered at the heavy wooden door. The king stirred out of his reverie. He had no servants here under the mountain, so he pushed himself to his feet and ponderously made his way to the door. The hammering sounded again as he raised the bar.

The king pulled the door open and saw a man dressed in deerskin standing there. He swept off an odd-looking fur hat that still had the animal's tail attached.

"I take it you're Barbarossa?" He stuck out a hand. "Crockett. The pilot said you needed to see me..."

"There are two of you?" the king demanded, his voice rising in outrage. "There are only a few thousand of those up-timers, and they have *two* heroes under the mountain?"

Crockett shrugged. "...and that I'm supposed to help you and somebody named Wenceslaus."

Frederick Barbarossa harrumphed. "At least that woman Earhart is more reliable than the Dutchman." He gestured toward the map on the table. "All of us are needed. Me, you, Wenceslaus. Arthur, although he has problems of his own right now. The Turks are coming."

Crockett shook his head. "I don't know any woman named Earhart. The pilot who found me said his name is Butch O'Hare."

* * *

Wilhelm Reuber whistled. "That is...quite good, Johann Markus. For *Die Nixe*?"

"*Ja*. She has agreed to an interview."

Both Wilhelm and Kaspar razzed him unmercifully for the rest of the day.

* * *

Sunshine still thought the house church was weird. Preachers rotated through a set cycle: Anabaptist, Arminian, Calvinist, Lutheran, and Roman Catholic. St. Mary's Catholic Church was a block away. First Baptist was three. Sunshine didn't have a deep interest in theology, but she'd gathered that the Arminians and Calvinists also had nearby options. Only Lutherans would have to walk any distance.

On the other hand, showing up every fifth Sunday for Catholic mass wasn't a big ask. She even hung around with the others for a bit afterwards.

"Hi, Eva."

"*Ahoj*, Sunshine."

Sunshine shuffled her feet. "You mentioned a prayer request once. A guy you work with, his boss's brother was missing."

"*Ano*, Casimir Wesner works for Georg Rudolph von Hessler. And one of von Hessler's brothers is missing."

"Not Hans Heinrich, I hope," a voice chimed in.

Sunshine turned to see Astrid Schäubin standing there.

"How do you know the von Hessler brothers?" Eva asked. "Through *Herr* Wesner?"

"*Nein*. NESS has met Hans Heinrich a couple times," Astrid replied, "*und* I know Hans Friedrich serves in the USE Army."

"This is a different one," Sunshine told them. "His name is Christoph. He's in Leahy."

"How did he...what is the expression? 'Wash up' in Grantville?" Eva asked.

"Oh, that's exactly how. I pulled him out of Redbird Lake a couple days ago. Hawker said they're still searching for next of kin. Do you think your friend could help?"

"Associate," Eva and Astrid said together.

"But, *ano*, I will go find *Herr* Wesner at once. Will you come?"

"I told Hawker I'd meet him at Redbird," Sunshine said.

"Oh? A date?"

"No, we're going to swim across the lake."

The State Library Papers
(1632 non-fiction)

Flint's Shards, Inc.

Movies And Television The Year Before The Ring Of Fire

Tracy S. Morris

Sometimes, I'd like to time travel to the day that I came up with the idea for Betsy Springer with my co-writer Brad Sinor and make her a little less rooted in late '90s pop culture.

It wasn't a problem when writing in 2009. But now, in the year of our Lord 2025, I have to first research the seventeenth century, then research the world of our shared universe, and finally, make sure that my character's slang and movie references are period appropriate. In the famous words of Doc Brown from Back To the Future: Great Scott!

It would be a perfect storm of research requirements, except that the movie The Perfect Storm was not released until June 2000, and the Ring of Fire occurred in April of 2000. So up-timers might be less familiar with the term.

With this in mind, let's take a look at the visual entertainment landscape up-timers would know in the year leading up to the Ring of Fire.

Movies As A Shared Cultural Experience

Let's say it's April of the year 1999, one year before the Ring of Fire. There's no Marvel Cinematic Universe, *Lord of the Rings,* or *Pirates of the Caribbean.* The Harry Potter franchise consists of two bestselling kids' books with a growing internet fanbase.

Betsy would be planning to go see *The Matrix* at the local movie theater. *The Matrix* was cutting edge for the late 90s and so transformative in both storytelling and visual effects that it would influence movies for years to come.

There is no *Rotten Tomatoes,* so Betsy hears about new releases based on what her friends like, as well as movie critics, reviews, and articles in magazines like *Entertainment Weekly,* her local newspaper, and television.

Most commercials for movies at this time showed clips with a voiceover narrative that explained the movie's setup, but not the plot.

But *The Matrix* promoted itself differently, using a very minimalist advertising campaign pointing to the internet. There viewers would see short clips of the movie that showcased the cutting-edge CGI special effects and the slick cyberpunk aesthetic. These served to convey the feel of the movie, not the plot.

The most well-respected movie reviewers up until then were Eugene "Gene" Siskel and Roger Ebert, a duo known for rating movies with a simple thumbs-up or thumbs-down. Although the word *meme* hadn't become widespread at this point, "two thumbs up" was a common saying, conveying that both Siskel and Ebert liked a movie.

However, Gene Siskel passed away in February of 1999. Roger Ebert would continue reviewing movies until his death in 2013, long after the citizens of Grantville traveled back in time. On March 31st, 1999, Ebert rated *The Matrix* a more traditional three out of four stars.

By then, seeing *The Matrix* had already become a cultural experience. Due to the limited number of outlets for entertainment in the pre-streaming era, everyone was watching and talking about it. If Betsy did not want to be left out of the cultural conversation, she would need to see the movie as well.

This wasn't a new phenomenon. Summer blockbusters have been inviting (nay, requiring) consumers to join in on the annual summer ritual of seeing the same movie and sharing jokes and catchphrases since 1975, when *Jaws* prompted people to say, "We're going to need a bigger boat."

But there was another reason why Betsy might have wanted to see a movie in the theater: attending movies in the late 90s was an elevated experience compared to watching them on television.

This was the last era of film stock before Hollywood transitioned to digital cameras. Film stock quality had improved to the point that movie colors were richer. And digital color correction hadn't yet gained a hold on the imaginations of creators. So even though 1998's *Saving Private Ryan* was desaturated as an artistic choice, most movies of the day weren't overly dark, or tinted blue and orange.

Digital special effects were also improving, which was how movies like *The Matrix* were able to deliver mind-blowing images like bullet time. *The Mummy*, released later that summer, was another movie with notable digital special effects.

This was the end of the era of director-led productions. In the '80s and '90s, directors like Stephen Spielberg, George Lucas, and James Cameron were the driving force behind getting a movie made. In the coming decades, it would be producers like Jerry Bruckheimer (who had already been an active and influential producer since he made *Flashdance* in 1983) and the now-infamous Harvey Weinstein (the Weinstein company was founded in 2005) who became the main drivers of movies. But the up-timers would not see that change.

The 90s were also the last decade of "bankable" actors: superstars who could propel a film into production and to number one at the box office on the power of their name. Brad Pitt was one such star. In 1999, he starred in both *Fight Club* and cameoed as himself in *Being John Malkovich*. Leonardo DiCaprio was another. In 1997, he starred in the movie juggernaut *Titanic*, and followed it up in 1998 with *The Man In The Iron Mask*. A third notable actor that year was Bruce Willis, who starred in *The Sixth Sense* in 1999, directly after starring in *Mercury Rising, Armageddon,* and *The Siege* in 1998.

The Sixth Sense was also notable that year for inspiring the saying "I see dead people."

Tom Cruise starred in both *Magnolia* and *Eyes Wide Shut* in 1999, then in 2001 (a year post-Ring of Fire) divorced his co-star and longtime partner, actress Nicole Kidman. *Eyes Wide Shut* was auteur director Stanley Kubrick's last movie, released after he passed away on March 7, from a heart attack.

Not to be left out, children's movies in 1999 included *Tarzan, Toy Story 2,* and *The Iron Giant.*

For the cost of a $5.00 movie ticket, Betsy got 2 hours and 16 minutes of superior visual and audio entertainment, plus clout for the water-cooler talk at *The Grantville Times* on Monday morning.

Seeing Movies As A Teen

During the '90s, teen movies were their own genre. Teenagers in the '90s spent a lot of time in shopping malls and their attached movie theaters.

This created a built-in audience for inexpensively made movies, and guaranteed a high return on the investment. Three teen movies released in 1999 (*Varsity Blues*, *She's All That*, and *American Pie*) cost $37 million to create and made a total of $393 million.

In 1999, Heath Ledger made his Hollywood debut in *10 Things I Hate About You*, a modern teen adaptation of Shakespeare's *The Taming of the Shrew*. This continued a trend of teen-movie remakes of classic literature that began with 1995's *Clueless*, a remake of Jane Austen's *Emma*. Another teen movie that was released in 1999 and based on classic literature was *Cruel Intentions*, which starred Sarah Michelle Gellar and Reese Witherspoon and was based on the 1782 novel *Les Liaisons Dangereuses*. *She's All That* was also based on classic literature, the George Bernard Shaw play *Pygmalion*, which was also the source for the musical and movie *My Fair Lady*.

In the following years, a number of factors led to a decrease in teen movies as a genre. Raunchy, R-rated movies such as *American Pie* excluded younger audiences, thereby slashing box-office profits. It also became more expensive to make teen movies relatable to their audience, due to quickly shifting cultural touchpoints in the internet era, as well as having to pay royalties to name-drop social media platforms that teens were using. Streaming services provided alternatives to movies, and teens in general found other places to spend time rather than hanging out at the mall.

Television Was An Inferior Experience

Part of why moviegoing was such an elevated experience was the comparatively low-quality image produced on a television and the higher price of an even moderately large set during this time. A new television in 1999 was a purchase on par with a washing machine or a refrigerator.

If Betsy's family purchased a rear-projection high-definition television in 1999, they would expect to pay $8,000 dollars ($15,500 in 2025 dollars) for a set with a 34-inch screen. While the set was advertised as high definition, that feature was limited to the very few shows broadcast in that format. *The Tonight Show with Jay Leno* was advertised in commercials for the Sony company as one such show.

A new television might be advertised as a flat-screen TV, but the screen was the only thing flat about it. The rear of the television sloped backward from the screen. Often, the entire set was larger than a one-hundred-gallon aquarium and required a special set of shelves to display it. A common piece of furniture sold in furniture stores during this time was an armoire-style cabinet to house the set as well as speakers, the video player, and any other media the family owned. The most popular model in 1999 had a silver-colored housing.

They were heavy, as well. A 32-inch screen might weigh more than two hundred pounds. Even if Betsy had the money to purchase the TV, she would need help from a friend to move it.

Weight, size, and price were all limiting factors in home televisions. Only as flat-screen technology reduced all those factors did large home screens become relatively ubiquitous.

Since older television sets lasted longer, the average Grantville home at the time of the Ring of Fire probably had an older set dating from the late '80s to the early '90s. Some homes might have had a newer set in their family room and an older set in a guest bedroom or basement rec room to use with a gaming system such as a Nintendo 64 or a Sony PlayStation.

Most of these were cathode-ray tube televisions (CRT). Models from the late '80s were square (4:3 aspect ratio), and less expensive models may not have had a remote control. Models from the early- and mid-1990s had a rectangular screen (16:9 aspect ratio). Nearly all had a remote control as a standard feature and may not have had exposed controls on the television set.

If a consumer had an older television without a remote, it was possible to route their television through their video home system (VHS) or digital video disc (DVD) player in order to use the remote from that device to control the television. Blu-ray did not come out until 2006 and took a few years to become really popular.

No Netflix, No Chill

Because Betsy is a movie fanatic, her weekend plans after watching *The Matrix* involve watching older movies at home.

In 1999, Netflix had been in operation for barely a year. Their business model at that time was based on shipping DVDs (Digital Video Discs). DVD players in 1999 were gaining a lot of attention due to the superior quality of a movie's video and sound compared to VHS (Video Home System) cassette tapes. Consumers were enthusiastic about the accessible menu and bonus features such as audio commentaries, documentaries, and deleted scenes. The bonus features were so popular that some VHS movies were issued with a limited number of bonus features, usually the deleted scenes, at the end of the tape after the movie's credits.

In 1998, fewer than 30% of consumers had DVD players. That jumped to 40% in 1999. A basic model DVD player cost around $200. Popular mid-range models by Sony cost between $400 and $700. A premium model by Panasonic could cost between $700 and $1,200 ($2,355 in 2025 dollars).

In the early 2000s, as DVD player prices went down, the superior technology replaced VHS in most homes. Many homes added a DVD player while still keeping their VHS to record television shows and play their existing library of tapes. In Grantville, at the time of the Ring of Fire,

DVD players were still more of a novelty. DVR (Digital Video Recording) devices like TiVo would be introduced in 1999, and would help homes to gradually phase out their VCRs for recording shows.

As of April of 1999, Betsy's family had only a VHS player, so she was stuck going to the local video store to rent VHS tapes. The VHS store in Grantville had one small section of front-facing DVDs to rent. The rest of the store was filled with VHS tapes.

The largest wall of the store was filled with shelves of front-facing new releases. Most hit movies at that time were released to home audiences six months after the theater premiere. A box-office bomb might have come out on home video sooner to make back its budget on the rental market. In this way, studios could turn a profit on their investment in the long-term.

In the '90s, there was also a robust direct-to-video market for movies of middling quality. For the prior decade, Disney had been releasing direct-to-video sequels to its most popular titles.

A couple of direct-to-video titles that Betsy might have seen on the New Releases wall were *Pocahontas II: Journey to a New World*, *Ernest in the Army*, and *Children of the Corn V: Fields of Terror*.

The most popular titles in a video store would have twenty forward-facing copies on the shelf. *Children of the Corn V* might have had two. As demand for a movie decreased, the store sold off older copies.

If Betsy couldn't find a particular high-demand video she wanted to see in Grantville, she might call a video store in a nearby town such as Fairmont to check if it was available there. But if someone beat her to that video store, she might not secure the coveted video. Some stores, though not all, would start a waiting list for a new release. Betsy's odds of getting her movie would have been better if there were a large franchise video store such as Hollywood Video or Blockbuster Video within a reasonable driving distance, due to their larger selection of new releases.

At the locally owned video store in Grantville, Betsy browsed the shelves for a half hour, then decided to rent *Titanic*. Again.

At the moment, there were several shelves worth of *Titanic* videos. Most of the time, all of them would be rented out. Tomorrow, they would still all be rented out. Next year, they would still all be rented out.

At over three hours long, the movie actually took longer to watch than the actual Titanic took to sink. The movie was split over two VHS tapes. The first was a feel-good historical romance. The second was a heart-wrenching disaster movie.

Other popular rentals that Betsy might have seen on the shelves included *The Parent Trap* remake with Lindsay Lohan (1998), *Spice World* (a remake of *A Hard Day's Night* with the '90s girl-power group The Spice Girls), *The Wedding Singer*, *Dark City*, *The Big Lebowski*, *Twister*, and *The Crow* (a 1994 film notable for being the movie in which Bruce Lee's son Brandon Lee was killed in an accident on set. The movie's aesthetic had a notable influence on *The Matrix*).

Besides posters for the latest releases, the video store would also have a poster with the slogan "Be Kind, Rewind." Failing to rewind your VHS rental before returning it often led to a fine on your account. Failing to return your video on time led to a much larger fine. By one estimate, Blockbuster Video, which was the largest chain of video stores in the United States in 1999, made most of their profits from unreturned-video fines.

The Start Of The Apple Revolution

When Betsy finished her movie, she would boot up her iMac to use a dial-up connection and a protocol called Telnet to connect her computer to her university's server so that she could use the Internet. Broadband internet would not become common until the early 2000s, several years after the Ring of Fire.

In this time period, it was common to refer to the Internet as a destination that one could travel to and return from. In later years, users came to think of the Internet as something that surrounded them, much like the atmosphere. Talk about user activity was eventually likened to visiting certain areas of the Internet, rather than the Internet as a whole.

In this way, an up-timer would have missed the Internet much less than someone from 2025. To the average up-timer, the Internet was just another place that was left behind, not something as ubiquitous as the atmosphere.

The common vernacular for using the Internet in 1999 was to "surf the net." Other slang terms for the activity included logging on or going online. The internet was also variously called the World Wide Web, or more simply the Web. By this point, "information superhighway" was already an outdated term.

Around 36 percent of people used the Internet in 1999. Like many other Internet users, Betsy received her first email account in college, and learned how to use the Internet at her campus computer lab. Many other users got access to the Internet through local service providers such as America Online (AOL), CompuServe, or NetZero.

Most people used computers made by Dell or Compaq that ran a Microsoft operating system. These computers had a tower or desktop, monitor, keyboard, and mouse. The monitor was likely a CRT. While LCDs were becoming popular in the late '90s, CRTs outsold them until 2003. Similarly, the mouse could have been an optical style, or it may have operated with an internal ball that physically moved rollers inside the mouse body. Betsy and most other journalists she knew used some brand of Apple Macintosh computer.

Apple had been a struggling company with a niche audience since the creation of the first Macintosh in 1984. Their largest customers were educators, journalists, and film production companies. This seemed to be due to Apple's focus on student and educator discounts, as well as supporting desktop publishing and special effects software.

For this reason, Apple computers were often used as props in Hollywood movies in the 1990s. In the 1996 movie *Independence Day*, Jeff Goldblum used an Apple computer to hack into the alien ship.

Betsy's computer was a brand-new "Blueberry-colored" Apple iMac G3. She'd only had it for a year, but Apple had already introduced four new models since it came out. There was no tower. Instead, the computer was contained in the same housing with the cathode ray monitor. This gave the computer the appearance of a gumdrop turned on its side. The mouse that plugged into it looked like a blue hockey puck. Laptops did not become popular until the late 2000s, in large part due to the technology advancements in the '90s that made them more user-friendly and affordable.

The revolutionary appearance of the new iMac provided a springboard to launch Apple in a new direction. Later products, such as the iPhone, would adopt the naming system introduced with the iMac.

Betsy had no idea how her computer worked. She just plugged it into the surge protector, hooked her phone cord into the modem inside of it, and turned it on.

She had to have a separate phone line to connect to the Internet, otherwise, if someone called, it would break her connection. When she connected to the internet, it sounded like demons being tortured. (Maybe, she thinks, they were.)

The Rise Of Online Fandom And Its Power To Influence Consumer Opinion

Betsy had been actively reading online fan-generated content about *Star Wars: The Phantom Menace*, which would release in another month (May 1999). Fan speculation and leaks were so sophisticated at the time that Weird Al Yankovic was able to write his parody song "The Saga Begins" based on no other information.

As is the case in 2025, popular movies and television shows in 1999 had an online fandom grow up around them. Science-fiction shows were more likely to have a large and active online fandom, as their fans were early adopters of computers and the Internet. Much of this activity centered on text-based discussions and fanfiction, due to the high bandwidth requirements of visual images. A webpage with many pictures could take several minutes to load on "dial-up" internet connections.

Early fandom activity started on private forums and email lists, usually hosted by universities on their servers, or on a bulletin board system known as the User Network, or "Usenet." The biggest *Star Wars* fan page then, as now, is theforce.net. At the time, it was called the *Star Wars Page* and was hosted at Texas A & M.

By the mid- to late '90s, activity migrated to free discussion boards and mailing list providers through Yahoo Groups. Fanfiction was often accessed through large, single-fandom archives.

Since this era predated online media organizations, online website content was hosted on free, fan-built and -maintained pages through ad-supported website providers such as GeoCities and Angelfire. Most of these pages were linked together in a chain of associated websites with a common theme, called "webrings." Web page addresses had to be typed by hand. The most common web browser was Netscape Navigator. There was no dominant search engine, though the most common ones included Ask Jeeves, Yahoo, AOL, Excite, Magellan, Hotbot, AltaVista, Lycos, Google, and WebCrawler.

Though science-fiction-based fandoms like *Star Trek* and *The X-Files* were among the largest genre fandoms online, fantasy and horror shows like *Buffy the Vampire Slayer* also had a sizable following.

Online fandoms migrated to LiveJournal and in the 2000s, but this occurred after the Ring of Fire event, so up-timers wouldn't know about it.

The *Harry Potter* fandom at this time was very niche, but was growing rapidly and contributing to the books' crossover success into the adult market. In October 1998, a 12-year-old Indiana homeschool student founded Mugglenet. The website grew along with the audience for the books. By the Ring of Fire, it had hundreds of thousands of fans.

While online attention could be a positive source for word-of-mouth marketing, it could also have a negative impact. When *The Phantom Menace* premiered, it developed a vocal online community based around hating the movie. This shaped *Star Wars* discourse throughout the 2000s and caused fans to remember the movies in a bad light.

Movie production companies at this point were embracing the power of the Internet. January of 1999 proved to be a pivotal moment in what came to be known as viral marketing when *The Blair Witch Project*, an independent film about a trio of film students who vanish under mysterious circumstances, premiered at the Sundance Film Festival. It made use of a campaign designed to fool the audience into believing that the events portrayed in the "found footage" documentary-style movie were real. By the time the creators admitted that the entire movie was staged, potential audiences were talking about the story, for a fraction of the price of a traditional advertising campaign.

The *Blair Witch Project* proved to be transformative in more ways than one. It revived the found footage genre and inspired the 2008 movie

Cloverfield. It is consistently rated as one of the scariest horror movies ever made. It's also famous for causing its viewers motion sickness.

But most of this notoriety occurs after the Ring of Fire.

Although it lies outside of the scope of Betsy's interests, it's worth noting that the peer-to-peer file sharing application Napster launched on June 1 of 1999. By the Ring of Fire, less than a year later, it would have an estimated 20 million users, but its life-span would be brief. After a string of lawsuits, it was forced to shut down on July 11, 2001. However it paved the way for digital music platforms such as iTunes, which launched in 2003.

Antenna, Cable, Dish And The Broadcast Experience

When it came to television, Betsy could rely on an antenna, subscribe to cable, or have a satellite dish installed. In the early '90s, the choice was largely determined by where a consumer lived, what programming they wanted to watch, and how much they wanted to pay for it.

Consumers in towns like Grantville might have access to cable, but not have the space for a satellite dish or large antenna on a roof, particularly if they lived in an apartment. Rural customers, on the other hand, might not have access to cable, but would often have the space to install a larger dish or antenna.

A television antenna was by far the least expensive method by which a consumer could watch programming. Many older televisions came with some type of built-in antenna, usually a pair of adjustable telescoping metal rods, called rabbit ears, or a metal hoop that attached to the back of the set. However, new televisions purchased in 1999 did not include an antenna.

Consumers could purchase an antenna separately and would usually make their selection based on the best type for their reception needs and location. Due to the hilly Appalachian area of Grantville, most consumers would opt for a rooftop antenna that would allow them to better receive signals. A long-range rooftop antenna in 1999 looked like a metal clothes rack and was usually mounted on a long pole. Some versions could be rotated to better receive a particular signal. Different types of antennas were better at picking up various frequencies, called Very High Frequencies (VHF) or Ultra High Frequencies (UHF).

After the purchase of an antenna, usually a one-time purchase, the actual broadcasting was free. The dominant broadcast format in 1999 was analog.

In 1995, many broadcast companies began transitioning from analog broadcast signals to digital, though the switch wouldn't be complete until 2009. Once a station had made the transition from analog to digital, consumers had to purchase a converter box for their television so that it could receive the new signal.

Television programming via antenna was free, though it was limited to broadcast channels (CBS, ABC, NBC, PBS, and FOX). The stations might be further limited by the antenna's ability to receive the signal in bad weather, or wind, or if the consumer lived in a "holler" (a colloquial term in the Appalachians for a hollow, a sheltered valley).

By 1999, cable and satellite TV services were becoming more popular due to offering a wider range of channels.

Dishes in use during this time ranged in size from three meters in diameter for older 1980s models down to newer eighteen-inch models that could be installed on a rooftop. Most satellite dishes were made of fiberglass or metal mesh. As dish sizes came down, their cost and installation were folded into the subscription price, allowing more people to afford this service.

By the late 1990s, cable and dish were direct competitors for consumers in many markets. The most common service providers were DirecTV and Dish Network.

As the name implies, cable was a television signal sent over coaxial cables. These tied directly into a receiving box which was programmed to allow whatever a subscription included and then relayed from the box to the TV. Often, in addition to the cable subscription, consumers had to rent or buy the box.

Cable was treated as a utility, with a down payment and monthly fee as well as a contract to rent the receiving box. Satellite billing was similar to a cellular phone, with a two-year contract. It was often provided through a locally-owned company.

The services were similar, regardless of type. Subscriptions granted access to a set number of broadcasting channels. Basic service would include about twelve broadcast channels. These would be the local affiliates of the major broadcasting networks, as well as the Public Broadcasting Station, CNN, and The Weather Channel.

Must See TV

The most popular shows of 1998 were all national broadcast network shows, which reflected that more people had access to these network offerings. These shows also had a greater impact, culturally, than shows on premium cable networks. NBC broadcast the three most-watched shows: *ER*, *Friends,* and *Frasier*. Their slogan for their primetime viewing block was "must see TV."

Friends would shape fashion and style choices as well as popular culture from the point that it premiered in 1994. A women's haircut, "The Rachel," was copied by millions of women after the actress Jennifer Aniston first wore it. The character Joey's catchphrase "how you doin'?" also became a popular saying.

In contrast to *Friends*, *ER* was a long-running medical drama with a large cast and a commitment to accurately portray medical procedure and protocol. The show helped to demystify the healthcare process, as well as increasing applications to medical schools. As with "The Rachel," George Clooney's Caesar haircut also became a fashion trend during this time.

Though the series concluded in 1998, *Seinfeld* remained culturally relevant. It centered around the fictional life of comedian Jerry Seinfeld and was billed as a "show about nothing." *Seinfeld* contributed many sayings to the national consciousness including *Yadda, yadda, yadda, No soup for you, Close talker, Puffy shirt, Regifting, Not that there's anything wrong with that, Double dipping,* and many, many more. *Seinfeld* also invented and popularized Festivus, a secular alternative to Christmas.

In the fall of 1999, *Who Wants To Be A Millionaire* would debut, reviving the game-show format. The show would take the top three spots in the Nielsen ratings. The catchphrases "That's my final answer" and "I'd like to phone a friend" would be some of the last twentieth-century sayings that the up-timers would learn.

FOX broadcasting was still airing *The X-Files*, a science-fiction mystery drama about conspiracy theorist/FBI investigator Fox Mulder and his skeptical partner, Doctor Dana Scully. The show was part of the cultural landscape of the '90s. Thanks to the show, mysteries of supernatural origin in real life were often referred to as X-Files. Believers might be called "Mulder," while skeptics might be called "Scully." Even the opening bars of the show's introduction could be whistled to indicate that the whistler found a situation to be creepy. By 1999, however, the quality of the show was much diminished from the early seasons.

The X-Files is also known for what anthropologists have termed "The Scully Effect," in which the popularity of FBI agent and medical doctor Dana Scully led many young women to join STEM fields.

FOX had also been airing *The Simpsons* for a decade by this point. Many fans and critics argue that 1999 was the peak of the show's quality. Even people who didn't watch the show might use Homer Simpson's catch-phrase, "D'oh!"

Warner Brothers had a network focused on youth-oriented program-ming, called The WB. The most notable shows on The WB were *Buffy the Vampire Slayer*, *Angel*, *Felicity*, *Charmed*, and *Dawson's Creek*.

Of these, *Buffy the Vampire Slayer* was the most culturally significant. The show, which premiered in 1997 as a serious reimagining of an earlier movie about a cheerleader who fought vampires, was novel at the time. It immediately imprinted itself on the public consciousness to the point that any female warrior might be called "Buffy."

The show was also known for its unique dialog, which became known as "Buffy-speak." Buffy-speak was characterized by unconventional adjec-tival-noun structures, using "thing" as a shorthand word to describe items of all manner and size, adding -y to adverbs and truncating sentences. Buffy-speak both drew from and influenced language and popular culture in such a massive way that universities have devoted academic study to the phenomenon.

Other cable packages might include second-tier mid-price offerings with more stations, and a "premium" package with HBO (the Home Box Office channel) or some other prestige programming network. In 1999, HBO was known for its mafia-based TV show *The Sopranos* and its prison drama *Oz*.

Most higher-tier channels, such as Turner Classic Movies, filled ex-tremely narrow niches. TCM aired classic movies from the MGM Film

Library of over 3,000 pictures, which Ted Turner purchased along with MGM Studios in 1985. Turner courted attention while stirring up controversy when he aired colorized versions of classic black-and-white movies such as *The Maltese Falcon*.

MTV had already started to shift its focus away from music videos while still playing them on Carson Daly's show *Total Request Live*, which was often abbreviated to *TRL*. Non-music programming included *Daria* and the Claymation-animated *Celebrity DeathMatch*. *The Real World*, one of the pioneering Reality TV shows, had been airing since 1992. The most recent season as of May 1999 was set in Seattle. CBS's *Survivor*, which combined aspects of Reality TV and game shows, didn't air until May 31st, 2000. Up-timers missed out on this phenomenon.

Comedy Central had been airing the controversial *South Park* for two seasons at this point. Even people who weren't familiar with the show had heard the phrase, "Oh my God, they killed Kenny!"

The Cartoon Network's offerings included *The Powerpuff Girls*; *Ed, Edd n Eddy*; and *Courage the Cowardly Dog*. Nickelodeon celebrated its twentieth anniversary in 1999 with a televised special. The cartoon *SpongeBob SquarePants* premiered on May 1, 1999. The show would appeal to children and adults, but it would not have much time to make an impression on up-timers before the Ring of Fire.

Many television watchers would have one or two favorite stations. They would watch one station until a commercial break, then change the channel to watch the other.

A thirty-minute broadcast block typically contained eight minutes of commercials divided between two or three commercial breaks and twenty-two minutes of actual programming. Commercials were typically fifteen or thirty seconds each. Because this was a good time to leave the room for a snack or bathroom break, commercials would often be louder than the program.

The most memorable commercial of 1999 was a Budweiser beer ad that aired during Monday Night Football on December 20. In it, several friends called one another to ask "Whassup?" This immediately became a viral catchphrase that up-timers would probably use.

A strike by the Screen Actors Guild in 1999 led to the creation of an iconic mascot: The GEICO Gecko. Under the terms of the strike, advertisements couldn't use live actors. As a result, the insurance company GEICO created a CGI lizard. Their first commercial in August 1999 featured the voice of *Frazier* star Kelsey Grammer. In the commercial, the gecko calls a press conference to deliver a final plea that he not be confused with the insurance company. The gecko remains the mascot of the insurance company as of 2025.

Due to the nature of licensing and royalties, it was a common practice for broadcasters to air inexpensive box-office failures repeatedly as schedule fillers. Over time, those films became cherished childhood institutions. One such movie is *A Christmas Story*, which Turner Broadcasting aired through the '90s, eventually showing it on TBS as a twenty-four-hour Thanksgiving marathon beginning in 1997.

Other notable oft-repeated movies included *Clue*, *The Shawshank Redemption*, *The Princess Bride*, *The Three Amigos*, and *Hocus Pocus*.

The common experience of the time was channel surfing, the process of rapidly flipping from channel to channel until finding something to watch. This would have been the 1999 equivalent of mindless scrolling.

With all these channels, it could be hard to plan a TV-watching night. But the TV Guide channel broadcast a scrolling grid of each station's broadcasting schedule. Those lacking the patience for this could purchase a bound-paper *TV Guide Magazine*, which showed a week's worth of the grid along with a summary of each show.

With all these options—theater releases, VHS recordings, broadcast and cable programming, and the Internet—one might think that Betsy would always have *something* to watch. Unfortunately, that wasn't always the case. Sometimes she might have, in the words of Bruce Springsteen: "57 Channels (And Nothin' On)."

Available Now
The Muse of Music, Essen Steel, Essen Defiant

Flint's Shards, Inc.

The Muse of Music
David Carrico

When Italian musician Giacomo Carissimi hears about Up-time music in Grantville he sets off across the Alps to see and hear these wonders. Nothing will keep him from his dream of learning the new music and seeing new instruments, not even warring militias and the threats of plague. He shares the trek and what he finds in a series of heartfelt letters and several short stories.

https://www.baen.com/the-muse-of-music-2.html

Essen Steel
Kim Mackey

Who is Colette du Bois, why does Louis de Geer care about her, and what is her connection to Crucibellus? As the ripples of the Ring of Fire event continue to spread through Europe, new opportunities are created, new possibilities arise, and new destinies appear. Louis has a vision of one of those destinies, one that will change the Rhineland forever, but it will take some of the knowledge brought back from the future in Grantville to make it possible. And the perception, strength, and skill of Colette and her new up-timer husband may be the most critical piece of his plans. Soldiers gather, spies engage in espionage, and merchants wager fortunes on the slimmest of odds, in the hopes of bringing about a new future.

Published: 5/6/2025

https://www.baen.com/essen-steel-2025.html

Essen Defiant
Kim Mackey and David Carrico

Whether it was a blessed miracle or a disastrous catastrophe, the arrival of Grantville in Europe in the year 1631 created changes that are long-lasting and spreading wider and wider as time passes. In 1634, Louis DeGeer—statesman, merchant, and player of the game of princes—having extracted as much information and technology as he could out of Grantville, makes his move to establish a new state in the Rhineland, a republic that would draw on much of the political philosophy brought back through the Ring of Fire by Grantville. There are those in the westlands of Germany and the Rhine Valley who aren't happy about that. Louis' enemies draw on all the forces of the status quo to oppose his efforts. Louis discovers that it will take strength and determination, coupled with careful preparation and planning, to face them. And the ultimate confrontations will leave things up for grabs until the final moments.

https://www.baen.com/essen-defiant-2025.html

Coming Soon

Mrs. Flannery's Flowers, Gourmets of Grantville, Red Shield

Flint's Shards, Inc.

Coming Soon

Mrs. Flannery's Flowers, Gourmets of
Grantville, Red Shield

Mrs. Flannery's Flowers
Bethanne Kim

Big things are happening in Grantville since it was sent through time and space to war-torn seventeenth-century Germany, and up-timer nursing student Krystal Reed isn't handling it very well. She never wanted to live in Grantville and being sent back to the seventeenth century just makes it worse. Working with doctors who think bleeding is a legitimate medical practice and that women have no business in medicine is exasperating, to say the least—but their prejudices are no match for the new medical programs in Grantville and Jena. Now if only she can recover from losing her parents, her friends, her home, her college, and her future.

Nils Jorgensen and family are just a few of the thousands of down-timers looking for a new future in Grantville. They arrive with little more than their skills. Through hard work, the Jorgensens start a fashion empire.

For the elderly Irene Flannery, life is more about smaller, personal issues. With no family left up-time, her biggest worry now that's she's in the seventeenth century is having a married curate at the Catholic church. (The scandal!) But she has kept a secret since FDR was President and she'll defend her rose bushes to the death because of it.

Coming December 2, 2025

December 2025 Baen Bundle:

https://www.baen.com/w202512-december-2025-monthly-baen-bundle.html

Gourmets of Grantville

Bethanne Kim

There's a lot going on in the 1632 universe, just like there is in the real world. Sometimes, things are dropped into a story and it takes a few decades to follow up on them. The "cooking show" mentioned by Rebecca clear back in 1632, for example. If you ever wondered what happened to it, this book will more than answer your question! West Virginia may not be the first place that comes to mind when you think of foodies, but this is a whole new timeline and sometimes people get cravings. So what's a man to do when his wife wants a bagel with cream cheese over 200 years before they will be (were?) invented? If he's a really good husband, he hires a researcher to find recipes for bagels and cream cheese to surprise her on her birthday. Gourmets of Grantville isn't just about food, but food certainly takes center stage in this novel about life in down-time Grantville.

Coming January 6, 2026

https://www.baen.com/gourmets-of-grantville.html

Red Shield
Bethanne Kim

We take some organizations for granted. They have been there since automobiles were a novelty and few homes had the luxury of a refrigerator. The Red Cross, for example. Scouts for another. But what happens when you go back in time over 250 years and start a new timeline? How many, and how much, of those old institutions can you bring with you? How much will they stay the same, and how much will they change? Since Grantville is a small town, even if it has grown down-time, all the up-timers know each other, more or less, and some of them know how to use that to their advantage better than others. Red Shield shows regular people figuring out how to reimagine and rebuild the organizations they've known and loved to suit a new world they never expected to be living in.

Coming January, 2026

https://www.baen.com/red-shield.html

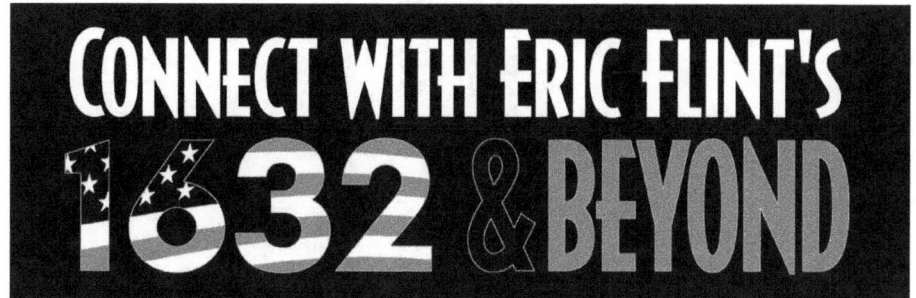

Connect with Eric Flint's 1632 & Beyond

We would love to hear from you here at *Eric Flint's 1632 & Beyond!* There are lots of ways to get in touch with us and we look forward to hearing from you.

Main Sites

Email: 1632Magazine@1632Magazine.com

Shop: 1632Magazine.com

Author Site: Author.1632Magazine.com

For anyone interested in writing in the 1632verse, or fans interested in more background on the series and how we keep track of everything.

Social Media

Our Facebook Group is our primary social media, but we do use the FB Page, YouTube, and Instagram accounts.

Facebook Group: The Grantville Gazette / 1632 & Beyond

YouTube: 1632andBeyond

Facebook Page: Facebook.com/t1632andBeyond

Reviews and More

Because reviews really do matter, especially for small publishers and indie authors, please take a few minutes to post a review online or wherever you find books, and don't forget to tell your friends to check us out!

You are welcome to join us on **BaensBar.net**. Most of the chatting about 1632 on the Bar is in the 1632 Tech forum. If you want to read and comment on possible future stories, check out 1632 Slush (stories) and 1632 Slush Comments on BaensBar.net.

If you are interested in writing in the 1632 universe, that's fabulous! Please visit **Author.1632Magazine.com** (QR code above) for more information.

www.ingramcontent.com/pod-product-compliance
Lightning Source LLC
Chambersburg PA
CBHW051436170626
46809CB00006B/2489